Anonymous

List of Diplomatic and Consular Officers of the United States

Anonymous

List of Diplomatic and Consular Officers of the United States

Reprint of the original, first published in 1868.

1st Edition 2022 | ISBN: 978-3-37504-675-0

Verlag (Publisher): Salzwasser Verlag GmbH, Zeilweg 44, 60439 Frankfurt, Deutschland
Vertretungsberechtigt (Authorized to represent): E. Roepke, Zeilweg 44, 60439 Frankfurt, Deutschland
Druck (Print): Books on Demand GmbH, In de Tarpen 42, 22848 Norderstedt, Deutschland

LIST

OF

DIPLOMATIC AND CONSULAR OFFICERS

OF

THE UNITED STATES;

TOGETHER WITH THEIR

COMPENSATION, PLACES OF OFFICIAL RESIDENCE, STATES WHERE BORN
AND WHENCE APPOINTED, AND DATES OF APPOINTMENT;
ALSO, LIST OF FOREIGN MINISTERS,
ETC., ETC.

DEPARTMENT OF STATE.

(CORRECTED TO AUGUST, 1868.)

WASHINGTON:
GOVERNMENT PRINTING OFFICE.
1868.

NOTE TO CONSULS GENERAL, CONSULS, AND COMMERCIAL AGENTS.

Officers in charge of the respective consulates general, consulates, and commercial agencies, are informed that the last edition issued of the "United States Consular Regulations" is that of 1868; and should any other edition be on hand in their respective offices, they will immediately report the fact to this Department.

LIST OF CONTENTS.

	Page.
List of Diplomatic Officers of the United States in Foreign Countries, and also Consuls General, Consuls, and Commercial Agents	5
Interpreters to Legations and Consulates	28
Marshals to Consular Courts	28
Judges and Arbitrators	29
Consular Clerks	30
Consulates General, Consulates, and Commercial Agencies, with their respective Agencies	31
Consular Offices of the United States, with the names of their respective Consular Officers	44
Commissions and Consulates General	79
Consulates General—Schedule B	79
Consulates General—Schedule C	79
Consulates General not embraced in Schedule B or C	79
Consulates—Schedule B	79
Commercial Agencies—Schedule B	81
Consulates—Schedule C	81
Commercial Agencies—Schedule C	82
Consulates not embraced in Schedule B or C	82
Commercial Agencies not embraced in Schedule B or C	85
List of Diplomatic Offices of the United States	87
Summary of Diplomatic and Consular Offices	90
List of Diplomatic Officers, &c., accredited to the United States	91
List of Foreign Consuls in the United States	95

LIST

OF

DIPLOMATIC OFFICERS OF THE UNITED STATES IN FOREIGN COUNTRIES,

AND ALSO OF

CONSULS GENERAL, CONSULS, AND COMMERCIAL AGENTS, WITH THEIR COMPENSATION, THE PLACES OF OFFICIAL RESIDENCE, THE STATES WHERE BORN AND WHENCE APPOINTED, AND DATES OF ORIGINAL COMMISSIONS.

[Consular officers at places marked thus *(a)* are at liberty to transact business.]

Names and offices.	Where employed.	Where born.	Whence appointed.	Date of original commission.	Compensation.
BRITISH DOMINIONS.					
ENGLAND.					
Envoy Extraordinary and Minister Plenipotentiary.					
Reverdy Johnson...........	London.........	Maryland.	Maryland.	June 12, 1868.	$17,500
Secretary of Legation.					
Benjamin Moran	London	Penn......	Penn.....	July 29, 1864.	2,625
Assistant Secretary of Legation					
Ed. C. Johnson.............	London	Maryland.	Maryland.	June 23, 1868.	1,500
Freeman H. Morse..Consul.	London	Maine....	Maine....	Mar. 22, 1861.	7,500
Thomas H. Dudley....do...	Liverpool......	N. Jersey.	N. Jersey.	Oct. 15, 1861.	7,500
....................do...	Leeds	....	....	....	2,000
H. G. Wells..........do...	Manchester.....	Ohio......	Mich.....	Jan. 28, 1868.	3,000
John Britton*.........do...	Southampton ...	Ireland ...	N. York..	Mar. 25, 1861.	2,000
Zebina Eastman.......do...	aBristol.........	Mass.....	Illinois...	Aug. 24, 1861.	Fees.
Charles E. Burch.....do...	aCardiff....	Penn......	Penn......	Mar. 4, 1864.	Fees.
Joseph H. McChesney.do...	New Castle.....	Ohio......	Illinois...	Jan. 22, 1862.	1,500
Alfred Fox...........do...	aFalmouth......	England..	England...	Mar. 11, 1863.	Fees.
Thomas W. Fox......do...	aPlymouth......	England...	England...	Mar. 3, 1823.	Fees.
E. G. Castle..Comm'l Agent.	aCarlisle.........	....	Dec. 24, 1868.	Fees.

* Naturalized.

6   LIST OF MINISTERS, CONSULS, ETC.

Names and offices.	Where employed.	Where born.	Whence appointed.	Date of original commission.	Compensation.
G. J. Abbott........Consul.	aSheffield.......	Mass.....	D. C.....	Aug. 1, 1864.	Fees.
Geo. M. Towle..Com'l Ag't.	aBradford.......	D. C.....	D. C.....	June 29, 1868.	Fees.
SCOTLAND.					
Wm. L. Duff.......Consul.	Glasgow.......	Scotland...	Illinois...	Sept. 29, 1866.	$3,000
James Smith*.........do...	Dundee.........	Scotland...	Illinois...	Feb. 24, 1863.	2,000
John S. Fiske ....do...	aLeith...........	Ohio.....	N. York..	Sept. 10, 1867.	Fees.
IRELAND.					
Thos. K. King......Consul.	Belfast....	Conn	R. Island.	April 5, 1867.	2,000
Edwin G. Eastman....do...	Cork..........	Maine....	Maine....	Oct. 16, 1862.	2,000
Wm. B. West*.........do...	aDublin....	Ireland...	N. York..	April 15, 1867.	Fees.
William B. West*.....do...	aGalway........	Ireland...	Wisconsin	June 22, 1861.	Fees.
Alex. Henderson......do...	aLondonderry...	Ireland...	Penn.....	Mar. 6, 1862.	Fees.
CHINA.					
Isaac J. Allen ......Consul.	Hong Kong....	N. Jersey.	Ohio.....	Nov. 28, 1864.	3,500
EAST INDIES.					
Nathaniel P. Jacobs, Consul General of British India.	Calcutta........	N. York..	Michigan..	Jan. 15, 1862.	5,000
Isaac Stone.........Consul.	Singapore......	N. York..	Wisconsin	Jan. 8, 1864.	2,500
Geo. A. Kittredge. V. Consul.	aBombay........	Mass.....	Mass.....	Feb. 10, 1863.	Fees.
G. W. Prescott...Com'l Ag't.	aCeylon....	Mass.....	Mass.....	Nov. 6, 1863.	1,000
....................Consul.	Seychelles	....	....	....	1,500
AUSTRALIA.					
Geo. R. Latham....Consul.	Melbourne......	Virginia..	West Va..	Feb. 25, 1867.	4,000
H. H. Hall....Com'l Ggent.	aSidney, N. S. W.	....	N. York..	Mar. 18, 1867.	Fees.
TASMANIA.					
Duncan McPherson, jr..Cons'l	aHobart Town...	G. Britain.	Tasmania.	Mar. 18, 1867.	Fees.

* Naturalized.

LIST OF MINISTERS, CONSULS, ETC.

Names and offices.	Where employed.	Where born.	Whence appointed.	Date of original commission.	Compensation.
NEW ZEALAND.					
W. G. Wright..Com'l Agent.	aBay of Islands.	U. States..	....	Dec. 1, 1866	$1,000
IN AND NEAR EUROPE.					
Horatio J. Sprague..Consul.	Gibraltar	Mass......	Mass.....	May 12, 1848	1,500
William Winthrop.....do..	Malta	Mass.....	Mass.....	Oct. 7, 1834	1,500
IN AND NEAR AFRICA.					
Nicolas Pike........Consul.	Port Louis.....	....	N. York..	May 29, 1866	2,500
Geo. Gerard...........do..	aCape Town....	France....	Penn.....	Mar. 21, 1867	1,000
Thos. Fitnam*.Com'l Agent.	St. Helena.....	Ireland ...	Dist. Col..	Nov. 28, 1866	1,500
Henry Rider...........do..	aSierra Leone...	....	....	....	Fees.
Thomas Brown......Consul.	aBathurst	....	....	Mar. 18, 1837	Fees.
NORTH AMERICA.					
Wm. W. Averell, Consul Gen. Brit. N. A. Provinces.	Montreal, P. Q.	Maine....	N. York..	Sept. 29, 1866	4,000
PROVINCE OF ONTARIO, DO-MINION OF CANADA.					
W. Martin Jones....Consul.	Clifton..........	N. York..	N. York..	Mar. 28, 1866	1,500
F. N. Blake...........do..	Fort Erie......	Maine....	Kansas...	Feb. 23, 1865	1,500
Thomas Allcock*......do..	Goderich.......	England..	N. York..	Jan. 30, 1866	1,500
Daniel R. Boice........do..	Hamilton.......	N. Jersey.	N. Jersey.	Jan. 30, 1866	Fees.
S. B. Hance...........do..	Kingston	N. York..	Illinois....	Nov. 11, 1864	1,500
James Weldon.........do..	Prescott	N. York..	N. York..	Oct. 15, 1864	1,500
Andrew W. Duggan*...do..	Port Sarnia....	Canada...	Mich.....	Sept. 29, 1866	1,500
D. Thurston...........do..	Toronto........	Mass.....	Mass.....	Oct. 14, 1864	1,500
Andrew J. Stevens.....do..	Windsor........	N. York..	Iowa.....	Sept. 29, 1866	1,500

* Naturalized.

LIST OF MINISTERS, CONSULS, ETC.

Names and offices.	Where employed.	Where born.	Whence appointed.	Date of original commission.	Compensation.
PROVINCE OF QUEBEC, DOMINION OF CANADA.					
Chas. H. Powers....Consul.	Coaticook	N. H	N. H	Oct. 14, 1864	$1,500
H. Le Boutillier ....do..	aGaspé Basin ...	....	....	Mar. 18, 1867	Fees.
Chas. Robinson........do..	Quebec........	Vermont .	Vermont .	Mar. 24, 1868	1,500
L. P. Blodgett.........do..	St. John's	Vermont .	Vermont .	May 4, 1866	1,500
PROVINCE OF NOVA SCOTIA, DOMINION OF CANADA.					
Mortimer M. Jackson.Consul.	Halifax	N. York..	Wis.....	Aug. 1, 1861	2,000
Benjamin H. Norton....do..	Pictou.........	Mass	Mass	July 12, 1842	1,500
PROVINCE OF NEW BRUNSWICK, DOMINION OF CANADA.					
Darius B. Warner...Consul.	aSt. John.......	Ohio.....	Ohio.....	May 4, 1866	Fees.
NEW FOUNDLAND.					
Thos. N. Molloy* ...Consul.	aSt. John's	N. F.....	N. York..	Mar. 18, 1867	Fees.
PRINCE EDWARD ISLAND.					
E. P. Scammon.....Consul.	Charlottetown..	Maine....	Ohio.....	May 4, 1866	1,500
BRITISH COLUMBIA.					
Allen Francis.......Consul.	aVictoria, V. I...	Conn	Illinois...	Nov. 11, 1861	Fees.
WEST INDIES.					
Aaron Gregg ....Consul.	Kingston, Jamaica.	Ky.....	Tenn	July 15, 1865	2,000
Thomas Kirkpatrick....do..	Nassau, N. P...	N. York..	N. York..	June 20, 1864	2,000
Oliver Mungen..........do..	Turk's Islands .	....	Ohio.....	June 6, 1868	2,000
Jos. G. Morton.........do..	aBarbadoes	Conn	Conn	April 10, 1866	Fees.
....do..	aTrinidad	....	....	....	Fees.
Charles M. Allen.......do..	aBermuda	Mass	N. York..	Aug. 7, 1861	Fees.

* Naturalized.

LIST OF MINISTERS, CONSULS, ETC.

9

Names and offices.	Where employed.	Where born.	Whence appointed.	Date of original commission.	Compensation.
H. A. Arrindell.Com'l Agent.	aAntigua......	....	....	Oct. 1, 1867	Fees.
Emile S. Delisle ....do..	aSt. Christopher.	U. S.....	St. Christopher.	Aug. 16, 1859	Fees.
.... do..	aBelize...............	....	....	....	Fees.
SOUTH AMERICA.					
P. Figyelmesy*.....Consul.	Demerara	Hungary .	Dist. Col.	Jan. 30, 1865	$2,000
FALKLAND ISLANDS.					
...............Com'l Agent.	aPort Stanley...	....	....	....	1,000
RUSSIA.					
Envoy Extraordinary and Minister Plenipotentiary.					
Cassius M. Clay	St. Petersburg..	Ky	Ky	Mar. 11, 1863	12,000
Secretary of Legation.					
Jeremiah Curtin	St. Petersburg..	Mich	Wis	Nov. 14, 1864	1,800
Geo. Pomutz*......Consul.	St. Petersburg..	Hungary .	Iowa	Feb. 16, 1866	2,000
Eugene Schuyler ......do..	Moscow	N. York..	N. York..	July 15, 1867	2,000
Timothy C. Smith......do..	Odessa	Vermont .	Vermont .	June 1, 1861	2,000
Henry B. Stacy........do..	Revel	Vermont .	Vermont .	Aug. 10, 1861	2,000
Perry McD. Collins.C. Ag't.	aAmoor River...	N. York..	Cal......	Sept. 10, 1861	1,000
A. Schwartz........Consul.	aRiga	Russia ...	Russia ...	Nov. 24, 1862	Fees.
Edmundt Brandt.......do..	aArchangel	Russia ...	Russia ...	June 21, 1832	Fees.
Reynold Frenckell .....do..	aHelsingfors	Finland ..	Finland ..	Aug. 31, 1850	Fees.
FRENCH DOMINIONS.					
Envoy Extraordinary and Minister Plenipotentiary.					
John A Dix	Paris..........	N. H	N. York..	Sept. 24, 1866	17,500

* Naturalized.

2

10 LIST OF MINISTERS, CONSULS, ETC.

Names and offices.	Where employed.	Where born.	Whence appointed.	Date of original commission.	Compensation.
Secretary of Legation.					
Wickham Hoffman.........	Paris..........	N. York..	La	Mar. 22, 1865	$2,625
Assistant Secretary of Legation.					
John W. Dix...............	Paris........	....	N. York..	Mar. 18, 1867	1,500
John G. Nicolay* ...Consul.	Paris..........	Germany.	Illinois...	May 31, 1865	5,000
Dwight Morris ....do..	Havre.........	Conn	Conn	June 18, 1866	6,000
Martin F. Conway .....do..	Marseilles	Md	Virginia..	June 30, 1866	2,500
Wm. E. Gleeson........do..	Bordeaux	Md	Dakota ..	June 18, 1866	2,000
Edw'd Robinson........do..	Strasbourg	Mass	N. York..	April 26, 1866	Fees.
Thomas P. Smith ......do..	La Rochelle ...	Mass	Mass	Mar. 11, 1865	1,500
P. J. Osterhaus*.......do..	Lyons.........	Russia ...	Missouri .	June 18, 1866	2,000
John de la Montagnie ..do..	Boulogne......	N. York..	N. York..	Sept. 25, 1865	1,500
......................do..	Nantes	....	....	....	1,500
John W. McClure......do..	aNapoléon Vendée.	Penn	N. York..	June 27, 1866	Fees.
Asa O. Aldis ....do..	Nice	Vermont .	Vermont .	Sept. 15, 1865	1,500
A. G. Gill.............do..	aReims..........	N. York..	N. York..	Mar. 1, 1867	Fees.
WEST INDIES.					
...................Consul.	aMartinique	....	....	....	1,500
H. Thionville..........do..	aGuadaloupe....	G u a d a-loupe.	G u a d a-loupe.	May 18, 1864	Fees.
AFRICA.					
E. L. Kingsbury....Consul.	aAlgiers	Maine....	Maine....	Feb. 19, 1863	1,500
Aug. Perrot ...Com'l Agent.	aGaboon	N. York..	Penn	April 23, 1866	1,000
AMERICA.					
...................Consul.	aCayenne......	....	....	....	Fees.

* Naturalized.

LIST OF MINISTERS, CONSULS, ETC.

11

Names and offices.	Where employed.	Where born.	Whence appointed.	Date of original commission.	Compensation.
Jno. P. Frecker.Com'l Agent.	aSt. Pierre, Miquelon.	Canada...	St. Pierre.	May 7, 1864	Fees.

SPANISH DOMINIONS.

Envoy Extraordinary and Minister Plenipotentiary.

John P. Hale............	Madrid........	....	N. H.....	Mar. 15, 1865	$12,000

Secretary of Legation.

Horatio J. Perry...........	Madrid........	N. H.....	N. H.....	April 30, 1861	1,800
R. F. Farrell*.. ....Consul.	Cadiz........	Ireland...	Ohio.....	Aug. 10, 1865	1,500
A. M. Hancock........do...	Malaga........	Ky.......	Ky.......	April 18, 1861	1,500
John A. Little........do...	Barcelona......	Mass.....	Mass.....	June 21, 1861	1,500
Houghton B. Robinson.do...	Port Mahon....	Penn.....	Penn.....	Feb. 14, 1862	1,500
...................do...	aValencia.......	....	....	....	Fees.
Lorenzo Dahl*........do...	aBilbao.........	Norway..	U. S.....	Mar. 18, 1867	Fees.
Louis Gallo...........do...	aSantander......	....	....	Mar. 18, 1867	Fees.
John Cunningham.....do...	aSeville........	Scotland..	Spain	June 24, 1859	Fees.
John Morand.........do...	aDenia........	....	Spain	May 11, 1852	Fees.
Manuel Barcena.......do...	aVigo	Spain	Spain	Sept. 17, 1861	Fees.
William L. Giro.......do...	aAlicante	....	Spain	Jan. 20, 1853	Fees.
Cirilo Molina.........do...	aCarthagena	....	Spain	Nov. 25, 1862	Fees.

CUBA.

...........Consul Gen'l.	Havana........	....	....	....	6,000
Henry C. Hall......Consul.	Matanzas	Conn.....	N. York..	Mar. 18, 1864	2,500
F. F. Cavada*........do...	Trinidad de Cuba.	Cuba.....	Penn.....	Sept. 6, 1865	2,500
Elisha F. Wallace.....do...	Santiago de Cuba.	N. H.....	N. York..	Aug. 10, 1861	2,500

* Naturalized.

12 LIST OF MINISTERS, CONSULS, ETC.

Names and offices.	Where employed.	Where born.	Whence appointed.	Date of original commission.	Compensation.
PORTO RICO.					
A. Jordan*.........Consul.	San Juan......	France...	Penn.....	Mar. 20, 1867	$2,000
OTHER SPANISH ISLANDS.					
Wm. H. Dabney†...Consul.	aTeneriffe.......	Fayal....	R. Island.	Jan. 22, 1862	Fees.
J. B. Pearson|.........do...	aManilla.........	... .	... .	Mar. 18, 1867	Fees.
PORTUGUESE DOMIN-IONS.					
Minister Resident.					
James E. Harvey...........	Lisbon..........	S. C.....	Penn.....	Mar. 28, 1861	....
Secretary of Legation.					
....	Lisbon..........	....	....	....	1,500
Charles A. Monrot..Consul.	Lisbon..........	Lisbon...	N. York..	Nov. 4, 1861	1,500
Henry W. Diman.....do...	Oporto	R. Island.	R. Island.	June 14, 1862	1,500
Charles A. Leas.......do...	Funchal	Md	Md	Mar. 15, 1865	1,500
Charles W. Dabney...do...	aFayal, Azores..	Mass.....	Mass.....	Aug. 6, 1846	750
Benj. Tripp, jr.........do...	aSantiago, Cape Verde.	Mass.....	Mass.....	July 20, 1867	750
.....................do...	aMacao	... .	... .	....	Fees.
.....................do...	aBissao	... .	... .	....	Fees.
Augustus A. Silva*..Com. Ag't	aSt. Paul de Lo-ando.	Brazil....	Mass.....	May 14, 1864	1,000
D. L. Marsins......Consul.	aSt. Thomé	... .	... .	April 12, 1867	Fees.
Caleb Cooke..........do...	aMozambique....	... .	Mass.....	Mar. 3, 1865	Fees.
BELGIUM.					
Minister Resident.					
Henry S. Sanford...........	Brussels.......	Conn.....	Conn.....	Mar. 20, 1861	7,500

* Naturalized. † Of American parents residing temporarily abroad.

LIST OF MINISTERS CONSULS, ETC.

Names and offices.	Where employed.	Where born.	Whence appointed.	Date of original commission.	Compensation.
Secretary of Legation.					
Aaron Goodrich............	Brussels.......	N. York..	Minn.....	Mar. 26, 1861	$1,500
John Wilson........Consul.	Antwerp........	Penn.....	Penn.....	Nov. 11, 1865	2,000
......................do..	aGhent...........	....	....	....	Fees.
Arthur Genaert ....do..	aLiege..........	Belgium..	Belgium..	Mar. 18, 1867	Fees.
......................do..	aBrussels.......	....	....	....	Fees.
......................do..	aVerviers.......	....	....	....	Fees.
M. Van J. Duclos......do..	Ostend	....	....	Mar. 18, 1867	Fees.
DOMINIONS OF THE NETHERLANDS.					
Minister Resident.					
Hugh Ewing..............	The Hague.....	Ohio.....	Kansas...	Sept. 24, 1866	7,500
Secretary of Legation.					
....	The Hague.....	....	....	....	1,500
Albert Rhodes ......Consul.	Rotterdam	Penn	Tenn.....	June 30, 1866	2,000
Charles Mueller*.......do..	Amsterdam	Saxony...	Ohio.....	June 26, 1866	1,000
Stephen Higginson, jr...do..	aBatavia, Java..	N. York..	Mass.....	July 20, 1867	1,000
Henry Sawyer.........do..	aParamaribo....	Mass.....	Mass.....	June 14, 1858	Fees.
A. Von Gils....Vice-Consul.	aPadang........	....	....	....	Fees.
Charles Rey*.......Consul.	aSt. Martin	W.Indies.	N. York..	Dec. 22, 1858	Fees.
James Faxon..........do..	aCuraçoa, W. I...	Conn......	N. York..	Aug. 20, 1864	Fees.
DANISH DOMINIONS.					
Minister Resident.					
Geo. H. Yeaman............	Copenhagen....	....	Ky.......	Aug. 15, 1865	7,500

* Naturalized.

14 LIST OF MINISTERS, CONSULS, ETC.

Names and offices.	Where employed.	Where born.	Whence appointed.	Date of original commission.	Compensation.
Secretary of Legation.					
....	Copenhagen....	....	....	....	$1,500
...................Consul.	aCopenhagen....	....	....	....	Fees.
George P. Hansen*.....do..	Elsinore.......	Denmark.	Illinois...	May 2, 1863	1,500
Edward H. Perkins.....do..	Santa Cruz.....	Conn.....	Penn.....	Mar. 26, 1862	1,500
John T. Robeson.......do..	St. Thomas,W.I.	....	Tenn.....	July 1, 1868	4,000
SWEDEN AND NORWAY.					
Minister Resident.					
Joseph J. Bartlett..........	Stockholm.....	....	N. York..	Mar. 19, 1867	7,500
Secretary of Legation.					
....	Stockholm.....	....	....	....	1,500
Chas. A. Perkins....Consul.	aStockholm.....	Conn.....	N. York..	Mar. 19, 1867	Fees.
F. K. Bazier...........do..	aGottenburg.....	N. Jersey.	Sweden...	Mar. 18, 1867	Fees.
H. J. Lockwood ....do..	aBergen.........	....	....	Mar. 18, 1867	Fees.
Carl J. Kraby ....do..	aPorsegrund	Norway ..	Wis......	Jan. 22, 1862	Fees.
R. Burton Dinzey.Com'l Ag't.	aSt. Bartholomew	....	St.Thomas	Sept. 26, 1860	Fees.
NORTH GERMAN UNION.					
PRUSSIA.					
Envoy Extraordinary and Minister Plenipotentiary.					
Geo. Bancroft..............	Berlin..........	....	N. York..	Mar. 14, 1867	12,000
Secretary of Legation.					
Alex. Bliss................	Berlin..........	....	N. York..	June 10, 1867	1,800
W. W. Murphy.Consul Gen.	Frankfort......	N. York..	Mich.....	June 25, 1861	3,000

* Naturalized.

LIST OF MINISTERS, CONSULS, ETC. 15

Names and offices.	Where employed.	Where born.	Whence appointed.	Date of original commission.	Compensation.
Hermann Kreismann. Consul.	aBerlin	Germany .	Illinois ...	Dec. 18, 1865	Fees.
William Marsh* .... do..	aAltona	England .	Dist. Col .	April 22, 1862	Fees.
William H. Vesey ...... do..	Aix-la-Chapelle.	Penn	N. York..	Mar. 13, 1861	$2,500
Leopold R. Rœder* .... do..	aStettin	Wurtem- burg.	Wis	April 23, 1866	1,000
W. Colvin Brown ...... do..	aGeestemunde ..	Ohio.....	N. Jersey.	Mar. 2, 1867	Fees.
William W. Murphy†...do..	Hesse Cassel, Nassau, and Hesse Hom- bourg.	N. York..	Mich.....	Aug. 15, 1861	Fees.
SAXONY.					
M. J. Cramer* ...... Consul.	Leipsic	Switzerl'd	Ky	Mar. 2, 1867	1,500
William S. Campbell ... do..	aDresden	N. York..	N. York..	Jan. 22, 1862	Fees.
Henry B. Ryder .... do..	Chemnitz	Germany .	N. York..	Mar. 7, 1867	2,000
MECKLENBURG-SCHWERIN.					
Orrin J. Rose .... Consul.	aSchwerin	N. York..	Illinois ...	Sept. 25. 1867	Fees.
OLDENBURG.					
Henry W. Carstens*. Consul.	aOldenburg	Oldenberg	Mass	Mar. 18, 1866	Fees.
DUCHY OF SAXE MEININGEN HILDBURGHAUSEN.					
S. Hirshbach* ...... Consul.	aSonneberg	Prussia ..	Illinois ...	Dec. 8, 1864	Fees.
BRUNSWICK.					
W. W. Murphy ..... Consul.	aFrankfort	N. York..	Mich	Sept. 19, 1862	Fees.
HANSEATIC CITIES.					
Geo. S. Dodge ...... Consul.	Bremen	Vermont .	Vermont .	June 26, 1866	3,000
Samuel T. Williams.... do..	Hamburg......	Md	Md	Oct. 3, 1866	2,000
W. W. Murphy........ do..	Lubec, residing at Frankfort.	N. York..	Mich.....	June 25, 1861	Fees.

* Naturalized. † Residing at Frankfort-on-the-Main.

16   LIST OF MINISTERS, CONSULS, ETC.

Names and offices.	Where employed.	Where born.	Whence appointed.	Date of original commission.	Compensation.
BAVARIA.					
Henry Toomy* .....Consul.	Munich	Ireland ..	California.	May 31, 1865	$1,500
Geo. F. Kettell ....do..	aRhenish Bavaria	Mass	N. York..	Oct. 10, 1866	Fees.
W. Colvin Brown......do..	aAugsburg	Ohio.....	N. Jersey.	July 17, 1865	Fees.
Benj. Le Fevre ....do..	aNuremberg	Ohio.....	Ohio.....	April 20, 1867	Fees.
WURTEMBURG.					
E. Klauprecht* .....Consul.	Stuttgard......	Germany .	Ohio.....	Dec. 20, 1864	1,000
BADEN.					
Geo. F. Kettell .....Consul.	aCarlsruhe	Mass	N. York..	May 14, 1866	Fees.
HESSE DARMSTADT.					
W. W. Murphy.....Consul.	Frankfort	N. York..	Michigan.	Aug. 15, 1861	Fees.
AUSTRIA.					
Envoy Extraordinary and Minister Plenipotentiary.					
....	Vienna........	... .	....	....	12,000
Secretary of Legation.					
John Hay................	Vienna........	Indiana ..	Illinois...	May 20, 1867	1,800
P. Sidney Post......Consul.	Vienna........	N. York..	Illinois...	Jan. 18, 1865	1,500
A. W. Thayer.........do..	Trieste	Mass	N. York..	Nov. 1, 1864	2,000
SWITZERLAND.					
Minister Resident.					
George Harrington.........	Berne..........	Penn	Dist. Col.	July 7, 1865	7,500
Secretary of Legation.					
....	Berne.........		....	....	1,500

* Naturalized.

LIST OF MINISTERS, CONSULS, ETC.

17

Names and offices.	Where employed.	Where born.	Whence appointed.	Date of original commission.	Compensation.
August L. Wolff*...Consul.	Basle	Lippe Det-mold.	Iowa	June 19, 1861	$2,000
Charles H. Upton......do..	Geneva........	Mass	Virginia..	July 9, 1863	1.500
Charles A. Page ....do..	Zurich	Illinois...	Iowa	June 19, 1865	1,500
ITALY.					
Envoy Extraordinary and Minister Plenipotentiary.					
George P. Marsh...........	Florence	Vermont .	Vermont .	Mar. 20, 1861	12,000
Secretary of Legation.					
Henry P. Hay..............	Florence	....	Tenn	July 25, 1868	1,800
T.B.Lawrence.Consul Gen'l.	Florence	Mass	Mass	Mar. 27, 1861	Fees.
O. M. Spencer......Consul.	Genoa.........	Iowa	Iowa	Mar. 21, 1866	1,500
William T. Rice ....do..	Spezia	Mass	Mass	July 31, 1861	1,500
J. Hutchinson ....do..	Leghorn.......	Vermont .	Dakota ..	Mar. 21, 1865	1,500
F. B. Huchting ....do..	Brindisi	Bremen ..	Wis	July 27, 1866	1.500
Robt. L. Matthews.....do..	Naples	Ind	Ill	June 18, 1868	1,500
Luigi Monti* ....do..	Palermo ....`...	Italy.....	Mass :.. ..	Aug. 3, 1861	1,500
F. W. Behn*..........do..	Messina	Germany .	Kentucky.	Mar. 18, 1867	1,500
Wm. M. Mayo.........do..	aOtranto	....	....	April 8, 1867	Fees.
.....................do..	aTaranto	....	....	....	Fees.
C. Ribighini...........do..	aAncona	....	....	Mar. 18, 1867	Fees.
John Reichard ....do..	aRavenna	....	Penn	April 13, 1867	Fees.
Franklin Torrey.......do..	aCarrara	....	Mass	Feb. 29, 1864	Fees.
Francis Colton.........do..	aVenice	....	Illinois...	April 10, 1866	750

* Naturalized.

3

18 LIST OF MINISTERS, CONSULS, ETC.

Names and offices.	Where employed.	Where born.	Whence appointed.	Date of original commission.	Compensation.
PAPAL DOMINIONS.					
E. C. Cushmann .... Consul.	Rome	N. York ..	Mass	Feb. 6, 1865	$1,500
TURKISH DOMINIONS.					
Minister Resident.					
Edward Joy Morris	Constantinople .	Penn	Penn	June 8, 1861	7,500
Secretary of Legation and Dragoman.					
John P. Brown	Constantinople .	Ohio.....	Ohio.....	Sept. 23, 1858	3,000
J.H.Goodenow. ConsulGen'l.	Constantinople .	Maine....	Maine....	Nov. 13, 1864	3,000
Enoch J. Smithers .. Consul.	Smyrna	Del......	Dist. Col..	Mar. 11, 1867	2,000
Jeremiah A. Johnson .. C G.	Beirût.........	Mass	R. Island.	April 5, 1867	2,000
V. Beauboucher* .... Consul.	Jerusalem	France...	Dist. Col.	Aug. 30, 1865	1,500
W. J. Stillman .... do ..	aCanea	N. York..	Mass	Jan. 16, 1865	1,000
L. P. di Cesnola* ...... do ..	aCyprus........	Italy.....	N. York..	Aug. 8, 1866	1,000
N. Petrocochino* .... do ..	aScio	Turkey ..	Mass	Mar. 18, 1867	Fees.
.... do ..	aTrebisond	....	....	....	Fees.
MOLDA-WALLACHIA.					
Louis J. Czapkay* .. Consul.	Bucharest	Hungary .	California.	June 20, 1866	Fees.
A. Hartman .... do ..	aGalatza	Wurtem'g	....	Mar. 18, 1867	Fees.
EGYPT.					
Charles Hale .... Agent and Consul General.	Alexandria	Mass	Mass	May 18, 1864	3,500
George C. Taylor ... Consul.	aCairo	N. York..	N. York..	April 21, 1864	Fees.
GREECE.					
Minister Resident.					
C. K. Tuckerman	Athens	....	N. York..	Mar. 11, 1868	7,500
.... Consul.	aAthens	....	....	....	Fees.

* Naturalized.

LIST OF MINISTERS, CONSULS, ETC.

19

Names and offices.	Where employed.	Where born.	Whence appointed.	Date of original commission.	Compensation.
Matthew Megis ..... Consul.	aPiræus	....	Penn.....	July 25, 1868	$1,000
Amos S. York.........do..	aZante	Zante	Zante	May 22, 1853	Fees.
BARBARY STATES.					
Jesse H. McMath...Consul.	Tangier	....	Ohio.....	Mar. 26, 1862	3,000
William Porter ....do..	Tripoli	Maine....	La	June 19, 1861	3,000
G. H. Heap............do..	Tunis	Penn.....	Penn	Mar. 14, 1867	3,000
Judah S. Levy...Com'l Ag't.	aTetuan	Barbary..	Morocco..	May 18, 1852	Fees.
LIBERIA.					
John Seyes...Minister Resident and Consul General.	Monrovia......	W. Indies	Ohio.....	Oct. 8, 1866	4,000
L. F. Richardson.Com'l Ag't.	Grand Basaa...	....	N. York..	Feb. 28, 1868	Fees.
DOMINIONS OF THE SULTAN OF MUSCAT.					
...................Consul.	aZanzibar	... .	....	....	1,000
BORNEO.					
...................Consul.	aBrunai	....	....	....	Fees.
MADAGASCAR.					
J. P. Finkelmeier.Com'l Ag't.	Tamatave	....	N. Jersey.	Feb. 13, 1866	2,000
JAPAN.					
Minister Resident.					
R. Van Valkenburg	Yedo.........	....	N. York..	Jan. 18, 1866	7,500
A. L. C. Portman.Interpreter.	Yedo..........	....	N. York..	June 27, 1861	2,500
................Consul.	Yedo.........	....	....	....	3,000
Julius Stahel* ....do..	Kanagawa.....	Hungary .	N. York..	June 18, 1866	3,000
W. P. Mangum........do..	Nagasaki	N. C.	N. C.	Mar. 18, 1865	3,000
E. E. Rice.............do..	aHakodadi	U. States.	Maine....	Jan. 18, 1865	Fees.
T. Scott Stewart ....do..	Osacca & Hiogo	Penn	Penn	Feb. 10, 1868	3,000

* Naturalized.

20 LIST OF MINISTERS, CONSULS, ETC.

Names and offices.	Where employed.	Where born.	Whence appointed.	Date of original commission.	Compensation.
SIAM.					
J. M. Hood........Consul.	Bangkok	Mass	Illinois...	June 30, 1864	$2, 000
CHINA.					
Envoy Extraordinary and Minister Plenipotentiary.					
J. Ross Browne............	Peking	Ireland ..	California.	Mar. 11, 1868	12, 000
Secretary of Legation and Interpreter.					
S. Wells Williams..........	Peking	Mass	Mass	June 27, 1858	5, 000
Geo. F. Seward. Consul Gen'l.	Shanghai	N. York..	N. York..	Sept. 2, 1863	4, 000
Edward M. King.... Consul.	Canton	N. H.....	California.	Feb. 23, 1867	4, 000
Alfred Allen...........do..	Foo-Chow	Ky	Ky.......	June 5, 1868	3, 500
C. W. Legendre........do..	Amoy..........	....	N. York..	July 13, 1866	3, 000
J. L. Kiernan..........do..	Chin Kiang....	N. York..	N. York..	July 6, 1865	3, 000
Joseph C. A. Wingate..do..	Swatow	N. H......	N. H.	April 14, 1863	3, 500
G. H. C. Salter.........do..	Hankow........	N. York..	N. York..	Mar. 12, 1867	3, 000
E. T. Sanford ....do..	aChee-Foo......	Maine....	Maine....	Mar. 3, 1865	Fees.
..................do..	aKiu-Kiang.....				Fees.
Francis P. Knight......do..	aNew Chwang ..			April 5, 1867	Fees.
..................do..	aTien Tsin......				Fees.
E. C. Lord............do..	aNingpo........	N. York..	N. York..	Mar. 18, 1867	Fees.
HAWAIIAN ISLANDS.					
Minister Resident.					
Edward M. McCook........	Honolulu	Ohio.....	Colorado .	Mar. 21, 1866	7, 500
Z. S. Spaulding .....Consul.	Honolulu		Ohio.....	July 25, 1868	4, 000

LIST OF MINISTERS, CONSULS, ETC.

21

Names and offices.	Where employed.	Where born.	Whence appointed.	Date of original commission.	Compensation.
Elias Perkins.......Consul.	Lahaina........	Conn	Conn.....	Mar. 13, 1863	$3,000
....................do..	aHilo	....	....	....	Fees.
FRIENDLY AND NAVI-GATOR'S ISLANDS.					
Jonas M. Coe..Com'l Agent.	aApia	N. York..	California.	Mar. 9, 1864	1,000
SOCIETY ISLANDS.					
Francis A. Perkins..Consul.	aTahiti........	....	Conn	July 25, 1868	1,000
FEJEE ISLANDS.					
J. M. Brower..Com'l Agent.	aLanthala	....	....	Mar. 11, 1868	1,000
HAYTI.					
Gideon H. Hollister.Minister Resident and Consul General.	Port au Prince .	Conn	Conn	Feb. 5, 1868	7,500
Arthur Folsom......Consul.	aCape Haytien ..	N. H.....	Illinois...	Aug. 7, 1861	1,000
James De Long........do..	aAux Cayes	Ohio.....	Ohio.....	Aug. 6, 1862	500
Fred. W. Clapp.Com'l Agent.	aSt. Marc......	....	Boston...	....	Fees.
SAN DOMINGO.					
J. Somers Smith.Com'l Ag't.	St. Domingo ...	Penn	N. York..	May 14, 1866	1,500
MEXICO.					
Envoy Extraordinary and Minister Plenipotentiary.					
Wm. S. Rosecrans	Mexico........	....	Ohio.....	July 27, 1868	12,000
Secretary of Legation.					
Edward L. Plumb..........	Mexico........	....	N. York..	Nov. 5, 1866	1,800
Franklin Chase.Con'l Gen'l.	aTampico.......	Maine....	Maine....	June 13, 1863	1,500
E. H. Saulnier......Consul.	Vera Cruz	....	....	Mar. 2, 1867	3,500
John A Sutterch.Com'l Ag't.	Acapulco	....	....	July 22, 1868	2,000

22   LIST OF MINISTERS, CONSULS, ETC.

Names and offices.	Where employed.	Where born.	Whence appointed.	Date of original commission.	Compensation.
..................Consul.	aMexico......	....	....	....	$1,000
Jas. White............do..	aMatamoras	....	Tenn	July 27, 1868	1,000
J. McLeod Murphy ....do..	aTabasco......	....	....	July 20, 1867	500
..................do..	aPaso del Norte	....	....	....	500
J. Ulrich............do..	aMonterey	Penn	N. Mexico.	April 26, 1866	Fees.
..................do..	aCampeachy	....	....	....	Fees.
Isaac Sisson ....Com'l Ag't.	aMazatlan	N. York..	N. York..	April 19, 1866	Fees.
D. Fergusson..........do..	aSan Blas	....	....	Feb. 22, 1867	Fees.
Alex. Willard ......Consul.	aGuaymas	Penn.....	California.	Sept. 16, 1867	1,000
Ramon J. y Patrullo* ..do..	aMerida & Sisal.	Spain	N. York..	April 26, 1854	Fees.
..................do..	aTehuantepec	....	....	....	Fees.
R. C. M. Hoyt........do..	aMinatitlan	....	....	Sept. 10, 1862	Fees.
John M. Roura ....do..	aLaguna	....	N. York..	Mar. 13, 1863	Fees.
Charles Moye* ....do..	aChihuahua	Hanover .	Mexico ..	Mar. 18, 1867	Fees.
John H. Notiware......do..	aManzanillo	....	Colorado .	April 17, 1867	Fees.
Martin Metcalf.........do..	aAguas Calientes.	N. York..	Mich	April 24, 1862	Fees.
G. M. Prevost ....do..	aZacatecas......	....	....	Mar. 21, 1867	Fees.
F. B. Elmer...........do..	aLa Paz........	N. Jersey.	Missouri .	June 9, 1862	Fees.
..................Com'l Ag't.	Morales	....	....	....	Fees.
Wm. Schuchardt. ......do..	Piedras Negras.	Hesse Darmstadt	Texas ...	Nov. 20, 1867	Fees.

NICARAGUA.

Minister Resident and Extra-
ordinary.

Andrew B. Dickinson	Nicaragua	N. York..	N. York..	April 18, 1863	7,500

* Naturalized.

LIST OF MINISTERS, CONSULS, ETC.

23

Names and offices.	Where employed.	Where born.	Whence appointed.	Date of original commission.	Compensation.
Secretary of Legation.					
....	Nicaragua	....	....	....	$1,500
B. Squire Cotrell. Com'l Ag't.	San Juan del Norte and Punta Arenas.	Mass	N. York..	Mar. 26, 1861	2,000
Rufus Mead .... Consul.	San Juan del Sur.	Vermont .	Vermont .	July 20, 1867	2,000
COSTA RICA.					
Minister Resident.					
Jacob B. Blair..............	San José	....	W. Va...	July 25, 1868	7,500
.... Consul.	aSan José	....	....	....	Fees.
GUATEMALA.					
Minister Resident.					
Fitz Henry Warren	Guatemala.....	Mass	Iowa	Aug. 12, 1865	7,500
Secretary of Legation.					
....	Guatemala.....	....	....	....	1,500
Edward Uhl .... Consul.	aGuatemala.....	N. York..	N. York..	Nov. 22, 1866	Fees.
HONDURAS.					
Minister Resident.					
Richard H. Rousseau.......	Comayagua	Ky	Ky	May 14, 1866	7,500
Charles R. Follin ... Consul.	aOmoa & Truxillo.	....	......	July 28, 1863	1,000
Wm. C. Burchard . .... do..	aComayagua & Tegucigalpa.	N. York..	N. York..	Oct. 2, 1860	Fees.
SALVADOR.					
Minister Resident.					
Alpheus S. Williams	San Salvador...	Conn	Mich	Aug. 16, 1866	7,500
John F. Flint ...... Consul.	aLa Union......	Penn	Penn	Feb. 14, 1868	Fees.
Ed. A. Wright......... do..	San Salvador...	Penn	Penn	Feb. 14, 1867	Fees.
J. Mathé.............. do..	Sonsonate	U. S.....	U. S.....	Feb. 14, 1867	Fees.

24 LIST OF MINISTERS, CONSULS, ETC.

Names and offices.	Where employed.	Where born.	Whence appointed.	Date of original commission.	Compensation.
UNITED STATES OF COLOMBIA.					
Minister Resident.					
P. J. Sullivan..............	Bogota	Ky	Ky	May 14, 1867	$7,500
Secretary of Legation.					
....	Bogota			....	1,500
Thomas K. Smith ...Consul.	Panama	Mass	Ohio.....	April 15, 1867	3,500
Francis W. Rice ....do..	Aspinwall	Maine....	Cal	June 14, 1861	2,500
Aug. S. Hanabergh ....do..	aCarthagena	N. York..	N. York..	June 8, 1863	500
E. P. Pellet.....Com'l Ag't.	aSabanilla	N. York..	N. York..	July 11, 1866	500
F. Davila Garcia.......do..	aSanta Martha ..	....	U. S.....	Mar. 28, 1866	Fees.
G. C. Crane ....Consul..	aBogota	....	....	Mar. 18, 1867	Fees.
Wm. H. Weir ....do..	Tumaco	....	U. S.....	July 23, 1866	Fees.
.....................do..	aTurbo........	....	....	....	Fees.
Nicholas Danies . ...do..	aRio Hacha.....	....	R. Hacha.	Mar. 7, 1859	Fees.
James M. Eder ....do..	aBuenaventura..	....	U. S.....	July 23, 1666	Fees.
..........Com'l Ag't.	aMedellin	....	....	....	Fees.
G. P. Gamba ....Consul.	aQuibdo.........	....	Colombia.	July 23, 1866	Fees.
VENEZUELA.					
Minister Resident.					
Thos. N. Stilwell............	Caracas	Indiana ..	Indiana ..	Aug. 30, 1867	7,500
Secretary of Legation.					
....	Caracas			....	1,500
Charles H. Loehr* ..Consul.	Laguayra......	Prussia ..	Penn	Mar. 16, 1865	1,500
E. Sturmfels...........do..	aMaracaibo	....	N. York..	April 5, 1867	Fees.

* Naturalized.

LIST OF MINISTERS, CONSULS, ETC.

25

Names and offices.	Where employed.	Where born.	Whence appointed.	Date of original commission.	Compensation.
A. Lacombe .... Consul.	aPuerto Cabello.	... ...	... ...	July 20, 1867	Fees.
John Dalton...........do..	aCiudad Bolivar.	... ...	... ...	Mar. 18, 1867	Fees.
Erastus C. Pruyn.Com'l Ag't.	Caracas..........	N. York..	N. York..	Mar. 23, 1868	Fees.
ECUADOR.					
Minister Resident.					
....	Quito...........	... ...	... ...	... ...	$7,500
Secretary of Legation.					
....	Quito...........	... ...	... ...	... ...	1,500
Elisha Lee......... Consul.	aGuayaquil.....	... ...	... ...	July 20, 1867	750
BRAZIL.					
Envoy Extraordinary and Minister Plenipotentiary.					
James Watson Webb	Rio de Janeiro..	... ...	N. York..	May 31, 1861	12,000
Secretary of Legation.					
....	Rio de Janeiro..	... ...	... ...	... ...	1,800
James Monroe...... Consul.	Rio de Janeiro..	Conn......	Ohio.....	Sept. 26, 1862	6,000
Thomas Adamson, jr....do..	Pernambuco....	Penn	Penn.....	Nov. 25, 1861	2,000
James B. Bond ....do..	aPara	... ...	... ...	Mar. 18, 1867	1,000
Richard A. Edes.......do..	aBahia	Md	Dist. Col.	June 12, 1865	1,000
William H. Evans......do..	aMaranham.....	Ohio.....	Ohio.....	Mar. 26, 1862	1,000
Aaron Young, jr ....do..	aRio Grande	... ...	Maine....	May 9, 1863	1,000
Charles F. de Vivaldi* ..do..	aSantos.........	Sardinia..	Kansas...	Aug. 7, 1861	Fees.
Benjamin Lindsey......do..	aSaint Catha-rine's.	Mass.....	Mass.....	Aug. 10, 1861	Fees.
Edward Burnett.Com'l Ag't.	Parnahiba	... ...	... ...	Feb. 11, 1867	Fees.

* Naturalized.

4

26   LIST OF MINISTERS, CONSULS, ETC.

Names and offices.	Where employed.	Where born.	Whence appointed.	Date of original commission.	Compensation.
URUGUAY. *Minister Resident.*					
H. G. Worthington..........	....	....	Nevada...	July 25, 1868	....
James D. Long ..... Consul.	aMontevideo	Md	....	Mar. 21, 1867	$1,000
ARGENTINE REPUBLIC. *Minister Resident.*					
H. G. Worthington.........	Buenos Ayres ..	Md	Nebraska.	June 5, 1867	7,500
Secretary of Legation.					
....	Buenos Ayres..	....	....	....	1,500
Madison E. Hollister. Consul.	Buenos Ayres..	....	Illinois...	Oct. 2, 1866	2,000
.... do..	aRio Negro	....	....	....	Fees.
Wm. Wheelwright, Com'lAg't.	aRosario........	....	....	July 26, 1867	Fees.
PARAGUAY. *Minister Resident.*					
M. S. McMahon.............	Asuncion	Canada...	N. York..	June 27, 1868	7,500
Secretary of Legation.					
....	Asuncion	....	....	....	....
R. C. Yates......... Consul.	aAsuncion	....	N. York..	July 23, 1866	Fees.
CHILE. *Envoy Extraordinary and Minister Plenipotentiary.*					
Judson Kilpatrick..........	Santiago........	N. Jersey.	N. Jersey.	Nov. 11, 1865	10,000
Secretary of Legation.					
....	Santiago.......	....	....	....	1,500
Ambrose W. Clark.. Consul.	Valparaiso	N. York..	N. York..	Mar. 16, 1865	3,000
W. W. Randall........do..	aTalcahuano	N. York..	Wisconsin	June 6, 1868	1,000
Charles C. Greene......do..	aCoquimbo......	....	R. Island.	June 21, 1860	Fees.

LIST OF MINISTERS, CONSULS, ETC.

Names and offices.	Where employed.	Where born.	Whence appointed.	Date of original commission.	Compensation.
PERU.					
Envoy Extraordinary and Minister Plenipotentiary.					
Alvin P. Hovey............	Lima	Indiana ..	Indiana ..	Aug. 12, 1865	$10,000
Secretary of Legation.					
H. M. Brent...............	Lima	....	....	Mar. 18, 1867	1,500
James H. McColley.Consul.	aCallao	Delaware.	Penn	Sept. 28, 1864	3,500
Raphael M. Columbus*.do..	aPayta	....	N. York..	Sept. 18, 1865	500
E. R. Sprigman........do..	aTumbez	Penn	Penn	July 17, 1868	500
.......................do..	aArica	....	....	....	Fees.
S. C. Montjoy ....do..	aLambayeque...	....	....	Mar. 18, 1867	Fees.
BOLIVIA.					
Minister Resident.					
John W. Caldwell	La Paz........	Ohio.....	Ohio.....	June 13, 1868	7,500
Secretary of Legation.					
....	La Paz........	....	....	....	1,500
Charles Milne ......Consul.	aCobija	N. Jersey.	....	Mar. 21, 1867	500

* Naturalized.

28

LIST OF MINISTERS, CONSULS, ETC.

INTERPRETERS TO LEGATIONS AND CONSULATES.

Names and offices.	Where employed.	Where born.	Whence appointed.	Date of original commission.	Compensation.
CHINA.					
S. Wells Williams, Interpreter and Secretary to Legation.	Peking	Mass	Mass	June 27, 1858	$5, 000
B. Jenkins...... Interpreter.	Shanghai			Jan. 24, 1865	1, 500
.... do..	Amoy			....	1, 000
C. F. Preston .... do..	Canton			April 25, 1868	1, 000
TURKEY.					
John P. Brown.. Dragoman and Secretary of Legation.	Constantinople .	Ohio	Ohio	Sept. 23, 1859	3, 000
JAPAN.					
A. L. C. Portman. Interpreter to Legation.	Yedo..........		N. York..	June 27, 1861	2, 500
.... Interpreter.	Kanagawa			....	1, 500
N. A. McDonald....... do..	Bangkok	Penn.....	... .	July 20, 1867	... .

MARSHALS TO CONSULAR COURTS.

Names and offices.	Where employed.	Where born.	Whence appointed.	Date of original commission.	Compensation.
SIAM.					
Austin J. Mattingly	Bangkok			July 20, 1867	$1, 000 and fees.
TURKEY.					
Alexander Thompson*......	Constantinople .	England..	N. York..	Aug. 16, 1861	1, 000 and fees.
Jos. Garguilo. Acting Deputy Marshal.	Constantinople .			....	1, 000 and fees.

* Of American parents residing temporarily abroad.

LIST OF MINISTERS, CONSULS, ETC.

Names and offices.	Where employed.	Where born.	Whence appointed.	Date of original commission.	Compensation.
JAPAN.					
Paul Frank...............	Kanagawa.....	....	N. York..	June 19, 1866	$1,000 and fees.
CHINA.					
Chas. Williams	Shanghai	....	....	....	1,000 and fees.
....	Han-Kow	....	....	....	1,000 and fees.
....	Chin Kiang....	....	....	....	1,000 and fees.
Benjamin S. Lyman	Foo-Chow	Vermont .	N. York..	June 9, 1862	1,000 and fees.

JUDGES AND ARBITRATORS UNDER THE PROVISIONS OF THE TREATY WITH GREAT BRITAIN OF APRIL 7, 1862.

Names and offices.	Where employed.	Where born.	Whence appointed.	Date of original commission.	Compensation.
Truman Smith.......Judge.	New York	Conn.....	N. York..	July 12, 1862	$2,500
Benjamin Pringle ......do..	Cape Town	N. York..	N. York..	Feb. 19, 1863	2,500
Geo. W. Palmer ....do..	Sierra Leone...	....	N. York..	May 4, 1866	2,500
Cephas Brainard .Arbitrator.	New York	Conn.....	Conn.....	Sept. 6, 1862	1,000
William L. Avery......do..	Cape Town....	Vermont .	N. H.....	Oct. 17, 1862	2,000
F. A. Whittlesey.......do..	Sierra Leone...	....	N. York..	Aug. 4, 1866	2,000

30 LIST OF MINISTERS, CONSULS, ETC.

CONSULAR CLERKS.*

Name.	Where employed.	Where born.	Whence appointed.	Date of original commission.	Compensation.
Albert J. de Zeyk..........	Lyons.........	Hungary .	Iowa	Feb. 7, 1866	$1,000
B. M. Wilson..............	Vienna	Penn.....	Penn.....	June 6, 1866	1,000
James Hand..............	Paris...........	N. Jersey.	N. Jersey.	Mar. 7, 1866	1,000
Wm. Heine..............	Paris..........	....	Dist. Col.	April 11, 1866	1,000
Thos. F. Wilson	Montreal	Penn.....	Penn	April 23, 1866	1,000
John M. Utley.............	Havana	....	Conn.....	May 25, 1866	1,000
L. W. Viollier	Liverpool......	Switzl'd ..	N. York..	Oct. 4, 1864	1,000
Burge R. Lewis...........	Shanghai	....	....	Oct. 1, 1866	1,000
Franklin Olcott...........	Paris..........	N. York..	N. York..	Nov. 7, 1866	1,000
A. C. Hyer...............	Callao.........	Penn	Penn	Nov. 29, 1866	1,000
Lorenzo M. Johnson	Jerusalem	....	Texas . ..	Sept. 12, 1867	1,000
Oliver B. Bradford.........	Shanghai	....	Penn	May 27, 1867	1,000
Aug. Glaser	Frankfort......	....	....	Mar. 23, 1868	1,000

* Thirteen authorized by act of Congress, approved June 20, 1864.

LIST

OF

CONSULATES, CONSULATES GENERAL, AND COMMERCIAL AGENCIES,

(Alphabetically arranged, with their respective Agencies attached.)

Consulates, Consulates General, &c.		Consulates, Consulates General, &c.	
Acapulco	Mexico.	Tutuila	Navigator's Islands.
Aguas Calientes	Mexico.	Archangel	Russia.
Aix-la-Chapelle	Prussia.	Arica	Peru.
Barmen	Prussia.	Aspinwall	United States of Colombia.
Cologne	Prussia.	Asuncion	Paraguay.
Crefeld	Prussia.	Athens	Greece.
Dusseldorf	Prussia.	Patras	Greece.
Alexandria	Egypt.	Syra	Greece.
Algiers	Africa.	Augsburg	Bavaria.
Alicante	Spain.	Aux Cayes	Hayti.
Altona	Prussia.	Jeremie	Hayti.
Gluckstadt	Prussia.	Bahia	Brazil.
Amoor River	Asia.	Aracaju	Brazil.
Amoy	China.	Bangkok	Siam.
Amsterdam	Netherlands.	Barbadoes	West Indies.
Ancona	Italy.	Barcelona	Spain.
Antigua	West Indies.	Tarragona	Spain.
Redonda	West Indies.	Basle	Switzerland.
Antwerp	Belgium.	Olten	Switzerland.
Apia	Navigator's Islands.	Batavia	Java.

32 LIST OF MINISTERS, CONSULS, ETC.

Consulates, Consulates General, &c.		Consulates, Consulates General, &c,	
Sourabaya	Java.	Berlin	Prussia.
Bathurst	South Africa.	Bermuda	West Indies.
Bay of Islands	New Zealand.	Hamilton	Bermuda.
Dunedin	New Zealand.	Bilbao	Spain.
Monganui	New Zealand.	Bissao	Africa.
Pau	France.	Bogota	United States of Colombia.
Beirut	Syria.	Bombay	Bengal.
Adana	Syria.	Kurachee Sinbe	East Indies.
Aintab	Syria.	Bordeaux	France.
Aleppo	Syria.	Bayonne	France.
Alexandretta	Syria.	Boulogne	France.
Caipha	Syria.	Calais	France.
Damascus	Syria.	Bradford	England.
Latakia	Syria.	Bremen	North Germany.
Sidon	Syria.	Bremerhaven	North Germany.
Tarsus	Asia Minor.	Brindisi	Italy.
Tripoli	Asia Minor.	Gallipoli	Italy.
Tyre	Asia Minor.	Bristol	England.
Belfast	Ireland.	Birmingham	England.
Belize	Honduras.	Gloucester	England.
Bergen	Norway.	Worcester	England.
Drontheim	Norway.	Brunai	Borneo.
Hammerfest	Norway.	Brunswick	North Germany.
Stavanger	Norway.	Brussels	Belgium.
Tromso	Norway.	Buenos Ayres	Argentine Republic.

LIST OF MINISTERS, CONSULS, ETC.

33

Consulates, Consulates General, &c.		Consulates, Consulates General, &c.	
Cadiz	Spain.	Newport	England.
Huelva	Spain.	Swansea	Wales.
Cairo	Egypt.	Carlisle	England.
Calcutta	Bengal.	Carlsruhe	Baden.
Aden	Bengal.	Ludwighafen	Baden.
Akyab	Bengal.	Mannheim	Baden.
Bassein	India.	Carrara	Italy.
Maulmain	India.	Carthagena	Spain.
Rangoon	Burmah.	Carthegena	United States of Colombia.
Calao	Peru.	Cayenne	Guiana.
Campeachy	Mexico.	Ceylon	India.
Canea, Island of Crete	Turkey.	Colombo	India.
Retimo	Turkey.	Madras	India.
Canton	China.	Chee Foo	China.
Whampoa	China.	Chihuahua	Mexico.
Cape Haytien	Hayti.	Chin Kiang	China.
Gonaives	Hayti.	Ciudad Bolivar	Venezuela.
Cape Town, Cape of Good Hope	Africa.	Clifton	Canada.
Mossel Bay	Africa.	St. Catharine's	Canada.
Port Elizabeth	Africa.	Coaticook	Canada.
Port Natal	Africa.	Stanstead	Canada.
Simonstown	Africa.	Cobija	Bolivia.
Cardiff	Wales.	Comayagua and Tegucigalpa	Honduras
Llanelly	Wales.	Constantinople	Turkey.
Milford Haven	Wales.	Adrianople	Turkey.

5

LIST OF MINISTERS, CONSULS, ETC.

Consulates, Consulates General, &c.	
Copenhagen	Denmark.
Coquimbo	Chile.
Caldera	Chile.
Cork	Ireland.
Crookhaven	Ireland.
Waterford	Ireland.
Curaçoa	West Indies.
Bonaire	West Indies.
Cyprus	Turkey.
Demarara	British Guiana.
Denia	Spain.
Dresden	Saxony.
Dublin	Ireland.
Dundalk	Ireland.
Limerick	Ireland.
Ningstown	Ireland.
Wexford	Ireland.
Dundee	Scotland.
Elsinore	Denmark.
Bonholm	Denmark.
Fano	Denmark.
Frederickshaven	Denmark.
Ringkjobing	Denmark.
Ronne	Denmark.
Thisted	Denmark.

Consulates, Consulates General, &c.	
Wyck-on-Fohr	Denmark.
Falmouth	England.
Scilly Islands	England.
Fayal	Azores.
Flores	Azores.
Graciosa	Azores.
St. Michael	Azores.
Terceira	Azores.
Florence	Italy.
Cagliari	Italy.
Milan	Italy.
Foo-Chow	China.
Fort Erie	Canada.
Dunville	Canada.
Port Bruce	Canada.
Port Burwell	Canada.
Port Colbourne	Canada.
Port Dover	Canada.
Port Rowan	Canada.
Port Stanley	Canada.
St. Thomas	Canada.
Frankfort on-the-Main	Prussia.
Funchal	Madeira.
Gaboon	Africa.
Galatza	Moldavia.

LIST OF MINISTERS, CONSULS, ETC.

Consulates, Consulates General, &c.

Galway ....Ireland.

Gaspé Basin ....Canada.

Geestemunde.....................Prussia.

Geneva ....Switzerland.

Genoa ....Italy.

Ghent ....Belgium.

Gibraltar ....Spain.

Glasgow...........................Scotland.

Goderich..........................Canada.

Gothenburg ....Sweden.

Grand Bassa ....Liberia.

Guadaloupe ....West Indies.

    Basse Terre, Guadaloupe. West Indies.

Guatemala ....Central America.

    San José de Guatemla.......Central

    America.

Guayaquil ....Ecuador.

Guaymas ....Mexico.

Hakodadi ....Japan.

    Sado ....Japan.

    Nee-e-gata ....Japan.

Halifax......................Nova Scotia.

    Annapolis..............Nova Scotia.

    Barrington.............Nova Scotia.

    Digby ....Nova Scotia.

Consulates, Consulates General, &c.

    Liverpool ....Nova Scotia.

    Ragged Islands.........Nova Scotia.

    Shelburne..............Nova Scotia.

    Windsor...............Nova Scotia.

    Yarmouth..............Nova Scotia.

Hamburg ....Germany.

    Ritzebüttel and Cuxhaven..Germany.

Hamilton ....Canada.

Hankow ....China.

    Kiu-Kiang...................China.

Havana............................Cuba.

    Gibari ....Cuba.

    Nuevitas.....................Cuba.

    San Juan de los Remedios.....Cuba.

Havre ....France.

    Brest ....France.

    Cherbourg...................France.

    Dieppe......................France.

    Dunkirk ....France.

    Honfleur ....France.

    Morlaix ....France.

    Rouen ....France.

    St. Malo....................France.

    St. Valery ....France.

Helsingfors ....Finland.

36 LIST OF MINISTERS, CONSULS, ETC.

Consulates, Consulates General, &c.		Consulates, Consulates General, &c.	
Hesse Cassel	Prussia.	Laguayra	Venezuela.
Hesse Darmstadt	Prussia.	Laguna	Mexico.
Hesse Hombourg	Prussia.	Lahaina	Hawaiian Islands.
Hilo	Hawaiian Islands.	Lambayeque	Peru.
Hobart Town	Tasmania.	San José and Pimental	Peru.
Hong Kong	China.	Lanthala	Feejee Islands.
Honolulu	Hawaiian Islands.	La Paz, San José, and Cape St. Lucas	Mexico.
Jerusalem	Syria.	La Rochelle	France.
Jaffa	Syria.	Cognac	France.
Ramleh	Syria.	Isle de Re	France.
Kanagawa	Japan.	La Tremblade	France.
Kingston	Jamaica.	Limoges	France.
Black River	Jamaica.	Rochefort	France.
Falmouth	Jamaica.	Sable d'Olounes	France.
Grand Caymans	Jamaica.	La Union	San Salvador.
Montego Bay	Jamaica.	Sonsonate	San Salvador.
Old Harbor	Jamaica.	Leeds	England.
Savannah la Mar	Jamaica.	Hull	England.
St. Ann's Bay	Jamaica.	Leghorn	Italy.
Kingston	Canada.	Leipsic	Saxony.
Belleville	Canada.	Leith	Scotland.
Gananoque	Canada.	Liege	Belgium.
Picton	Canada.	Lisbon	Portugal.
Napanee	Canada.	Belem	Portugal.
Kiu Kiang	China.	Cesimbra	Portugal.

LIST OF MINISTERS, CONSULS, ETC.

37

Consulates, Consulates General, &c.		Consulates, Consulates General, &c.	
Faro	Portugal.	Cette	France.
Lagos	Portugal.	Toulon	France.
Setubal	Portugal.	Matamoras	Mexico.
Sines	Portugal.	Mier	Mexico.
Liverpool	England.	Matanzas	Cuba.
Beaumaris	Wales.	Cardenas	Cuba.
London	England.	Sagua la Grande	Cuba.
Londonderry	Ireland.	Mazatlan	Mexico.
Lubec	Germany.	Medellin	United States of Colombia.
Lyons	France.	Melbourne	Australia.
St. Etienne	France.	Albany	Australia.
Macao	China.	Freemantle	Australia.
Malaga	Spain.	Queensland	Australia.
Adra Malaga	Spain.	Merida and Sisal	Mexico.
Almeria Malaga	Spain.	Messina	Italy.
Velez Malaga	Spain.	Catania	Italy.
Malta, (Island)		Syracuse	Italy.
Manchester	England.	Mexico, (city)	Mexico.
Tunstall	England.	Minatitlan	Mexico.
Manila	Philippine Islands.	Monrovia	Africa.
Iloilo	Philippine Islands.	Monterey	Mexico.
Manzanillo	Mexico.	Saltillo	Mexico.
Maracaibo	Venezuela.	Santa Rosa	Mexico.
Maranham	Brazil.	Montevideo	Uruguay.
Marseilles	France.	Montreal	Canada.

LIST OF MINISTERS, CONSULS, ETC.

Consulates, Consulates General, &c.		Consulates, Consulates General, &c.	
Moscow	Russia.	Odessa	Russia.
Mozambique	Africa.	Taganrog	Russia.
Munich	Bavaria.	Oldenburg	Germany.
Muscat	Arabia.	Brake	Germany.
Nagasaki	Japan.	Oporto	Portugal.
Nantes	France.	Aveiro	Portugal.
L'Orient	France.	Cacilhas	Portugal.
St. Nazaire	France.	Caminha	Portugal.
Naples	Italy.	Concelho de Boncas	Portugal.
Napoléon Vendée	France.	Espinho	Portugal.
Nassau	Prussia.	Figueira	Portugal.
Nassau	West Indies.	Leca	Portugal.
Green Turtle Bay	West Indies.	Ovar	Portugal.
Harbor Island	West Indies.	Paco d'Argos	Portugal.
Inagua	West Indies.	Peso de Regra	Portugal.
Newcastle-upon-Tyne	England.	Regoa	Portugal.
Old Hartlepool	England.	St. João da Foz	Portugal.
Sunderland	England.	Viana	Portugal.
West Hartlepool	England.	Villa do Conde	Portugal.
New Chwang	China.	Villa Nova	Portugal.
Nice	France.	Osacca and Hiogo	Japan.
Mentone	France.	Ostend	Belgium.
Ningpo	China.	Otranto	Italy.
Nuremberg	Bavaria.	Padang	Sumatra.
Bamberg	Bavaria.	Palermo	Italy.

LIST OF MINISTERS, CONSULS, ETC.

Consulates, Consulates General, &c.	Consulates, Consulates General, &c.
Girgenti......................Italy.	Plymouth......................England.
Licata........................Italy.	Brixham..................England.
Marsala......................Italy.	Dartmouth................England.
Trapani......................Italy.	Guernsey, (Island)........England.
Panama.........United States of Colombia.	Jersey Island.............England.
Para.............................Brazil.	Porsgrund......................Norway.
Paramaribo.................Dutch Guiana.	Christiansand..............Norway.
Paris............................France.	Port au Prince.....................Hayti.
Sedan........................France.	Jacmel......................Hayti.
Paso del Norte....................Mexico.	Port Mahon......................Minorca.
Payta..............................Peru.	Ivica Island.
Pernambuco.......................Brazil.	Palma......................Majorca.
Ceara.......................Brazil.	Port Louis.....................Mauritius.
Maceio.....................Brazil.	Port Sarnia.....................Canada.
Paraiba.....................Brazil.	Port Stanley.............Falkland Islands.
Pictou.........................Nova Scotia.	Prescott.........................Canada.
Arichat................Cape Breton.	Ottawa.........................Canada.
Cow Bay..............Cape Breton.	Prince Edward Island..........B. N. A. P.
Guysborough...........Nova Scotia.	Bedeque......Prince Edward Island.
Lingan................Nova Scotia.	Cascumpec...Prince Edward Island.
Port of Sidney.........Cape Breton.	Georgetown...Prince Edward Island.
Pugwash..............Nova Scotia.	Souris........Prince Edward Island.
Sidney................Cape Breton.	Puerto Cabello................Venezuela.
Piræus............................Greece.	Quebec...........................Canada.
Syra Isle....................Greece.	Chicoutimi................Canada.

40 LIST OF MINISTERS, CONSULS, ETC.

Consulates, Consulates General, &c.		Consulates, Consulates General, &c.	
Ravenna	Italy.	Aguadilla	Porto Rico.
Reims	France.	Areccibo	Porto Rico.
Revel	Russia.	Naguabo	Porto Rico.
Port Baltic	Russia.	Ponce	Porto Pico.
Rhenish Bavaria	Germany.	Vieque	West Indies.
Riga	Russia.	San Juan del Norte	Nicaragua.
Rio de Janeiro	Brazil.	San Juan del Sur	Nicaragua.
Rio Grande	Brazil.	San Luis Potosi	Mexico.
Porto Alegre	Brazil.	Santa Cruz	West Indies.
San José do Norte	Brazil.	Frederickstadt	Santa Cruz, W. I.
Rio Hacha	United States of Colombia.	Santa Martha	United States of Colombia.
Rio Negro	Argentine Confederation.	Santander	Spain.
Rome	Italy.	Santiago	Cape Verde Islands.
Civita Vecchia	Italy.	Brava	Cape Verde Islands.
Rosario	Argentine Confederation.	Fogo	Cape Verde Islands.
Roseau	Island of Dominica.	Maio	Cape Verde Islands.
Rotterdam	Netherlands.	Sal	Cape Verde Islands.
Sabanilla	United States of Colombia.	St. Vincent	Cape Verde Islands.
Saltillo	Mexico.	Santiago de Cuba.	
San Blas	Mexico.	Baracoa	Cuba.
San José	Costa Rica.	Guantanmoã	Cuba.
Punta Arenas	Costa Rica.	Manzanillo	Cuba.
San Juan	Porto Rico.	Santa Cruz	Cuba.
Guaymas	Porto Rico.	Santos	Brazil.
Mayaguez	Porto Rico.	Schwerin	Germany.

LIST OF MINISTERS, CONSULS, ETC.

41

Consulates, Consulates General, &c.		Consulates, Consulates General, &c.	
Scio	Turkey.	St. John	New Brunswick.
Seville	Spain.	Chatham and Newcastle	N. B.
Shanghai	China.	Fredericton	N. B.
Sheffield	England.	St. Andrew's	N. B.
Huddersfield	England.	St. George	N. B.
Nottingham	England.	St. Stephen's	N. B.
Sierra Leone	Africa.	St. John's	Canada.
Singapore	India.	Dundee	Canada.
Penang	Bengal.	Frelighsburg	Canada.
Smyrna	Turkey.	Hummingsford	Canada.
Dardanelles	Turkey.	Huntington	Canada.
Sonneburg	Germany.	La Colle	Canada.
Southampton	England.	St. Marc	Hayti.
Cowes	England.	St. Martin	West Indies.
Portsmouth	England.	St. Paul de Loando	Africa.
Weymouth	England.	St. Pierre	Martinique.
Spezia	Italy.	Eort de France	Martinique.
St. Bartholomew	West Indies.	St. Pierre	Miquelon.
St. Catharine's Island	Brazil.	St. Petersburg	Russia.
St. Christopher	West Indies.	Cronstadt	Russia.
St. Domingo	Hayti.	Wyborg (Finland)	Russia.
Puerto Plata	Hayti.	St. Thomas	West Indies.
St. Helena, (Island)		St. Thomé	Africa.
St. John's	Newfoundland.	Stettin	Prussia.
Cape Charles and Chateau Bay	Labr'r.	Dantzic	Prussia.

6

LIST OF MINISTERS, CONSULS, ETC.

Consulates, Consulates General, &c.	Consulates, Consulates General, &c.
Konigsberg...............Prussia.	Port Orotava, Teneriffe..Canary Isl'ds.
Memel......................Prussia.	Tetuan............................Africa.
Swinemünde...............Prussia.	Tien-Tsin..........................China.
Stockholm ....Sweden.	Toronto..........................Canada.
Gefle....................Sweden.	Cobourg...................Canada.
Strasbourg.....................France.	Port Hope..................Canada.
Mulhouse....................France.	Trebisond.............Turkey in Asia.
Stüttgardt...................Wurtemburg.	Trieste..........................Austria.
Swatow......................China.	Fiume ....Austria.
Sydney.............. New South Wales.	Trinidad de Cuba.
Adelaide..........New South Wales.	Cienfuegos.....................Cuba.
Newcastle.........New South Wales.	Zaza..........................Cuba.
Tabasco......................Mexico.	Trinidad, (Island) ....West Indies.
Tahiti.....................Society Islands.	Tripoli...........................Africa.
Talcahuano..........................Chili.	Tumbez..........................Peru.
Lota and Coronel..............Chili.	Tunis.............................Africa.
Tamatave..................Madagascar.	Turbo.........._.. United States of Colombia.
Tampico.......................Mexico.	Turk's Islands............. ....West Indies.
Tangier.....................Morocco.	East Harbor, T. I........West Indies.
Taranto...........................Italy.	Salt Cay, T. I...........West Indies.
Tehuantepec...................Mexico.	Valencia.........................Spain.
Teneriffe................Canary Islands.	Valparaiso..........................Chile.
Lanzarotte ....Canary Islands.	Venice ....Italy.
Las Palmas..........Canary Islands.	Vera Cruz.......................Mexico.
Palma ....Canary Islands.	Jalapa.........................Mexico.

LIST OF MINISTERS, CONSULS, ETC. 43

Consulates, Consulates General, &c.		Consulates, Consulates General, &c.	
Verviers	Belgium.	Windsor	Canada.
Victoria	Vancouver's Island.	Amherstburg	Canada.
Vienna	Austria.	Morpeth	Canada.
Brunn	Moravia.	Zacatecas	Mexico.
Pesth	Hungary.	Zante	Ionian Isles.
Prague	Bohemia.	Corfu	Ionian Isles.
Vigo	Spain.	Zanzibar, (Island)	
Corunna	Spain.	Zurich	Switzerland.
Port St. Mary	Spain.	St. Gallen	Switzerland.

A FULL LIST

OF

ALL CONSULAR OFFICERS OF THE UNITED STATES IN OFFICE, WITH THE PLACES OF THEIR OFFICIAL RESIDENCE.

[Alphabetically arranged.]

Consular offices.	Consular Officers.	Rank.
Aberdeen, Scotland	Alex. Brand	Consular agent.
Acapulco, Mexico	John A. Sutlerch	Commercial agent.
Do	J. A. Sutter	Vice-commercial agent.
Adelaide, Australia	J. W. Smith	Consular agent.
Aden, East Indies	Wm. H. Nichols	Do.
Adra, Spain	Ramon Medina	Do.
Adrianople, Turkey	T. E. Blunt	Do.
Aguadilla, Porto Rico	Ed. Kopisch	Do.
Aguas Calientes, Mexico	M. Metcalf	Consul.
Aintab, Syria	S. de Picciotto	Consular agent.
Aix-la-Chapelle, Prussia	W. H. Vesey	Consul.
Do	Chas. E. Dahmen	Vice-consul.
Akyab, Bengal	James Dickie	Consular agent.
Albany, Australia	Henry K. Toll	Do.
Aleppo, Syria	J. de Piccioto	Do.
Alexandretta, Syria	M. Levi	Do.
Alexandria, Egypt	C. Hale	Consul general.
Algiers, Africa	E. L. Kingsbury	Consul.
Do		Vice-consul.
Alicante, Spain	W. L. Giro	Consul.

LIST OF MINISTERS, CONSULS, ETC.

Consular offices.	Consular officers.	Rank.
Almeria, Spain	F. P. Roman	Consular agent.
Altona, Prussia	W. Marsh	Consul.
Do	Jno. A. Sievers	Vice-consul.
Amherstburg, Canada	Joseph Templeton	Consular agent.
Amoor River, Asia, (Nicolaefski)	P. McD. Collins	Commercial agent.
Do	H. W. Hiller	Vice-commercial agent.
Amoy, China	C. W. Le Gendre	Consul.
Do	W. P. Jones	Vice-consul.
Amsterdam, Netherlands	Chas. Mueller	Consul.
Do	A. Vinke	Vice-consul.
Ancona, Italy	C. Ribighini	Consul.
Do		Vice-consul.
Annapolis, Nova Scotia	W. R. Ruggles	Consular agent.
Antigua, West Indies	H. A. Arrindell	Commercial agent.
Antwerp, Belgium	John Wilson	Consul.
Apia, Navigator's Islands	J. M. Coe	Commercial agent.
Archangel, Russia	E. Brandt	Consul.
Areccibo, Porto Rico	F. Fernandez	Consular agent.
Arica, Peru	John T. Lansing	Consul.
Arichat, Cape Breton	J. G. McKean	Consular agent.
Aspinwall, United States of Colombia	F. W. Rice	Consul.
Do	Tracy Robinson	Vice-consul.
Asuncion, Paraguay	R. C. Yates	Consul.
Athens, Greece		Do.
Augsburg, Bavaria	W. Colvin Brown	Do.

46   LIST OF MINISTERS, CONSULS. ETC.

Consular offices.	Consular officers.	Rank.
Augsburg, Bavaria	Max Obermayer	Vice-consul.
Aux Cayes, Hayti	J. De Long	Consul.
Aveiro, Portugal	H. L. Feurheerd	Consular agent.
Bahia, Brazil	R. A. Edes	Consul.
Bamberg, Bavaria	Paul J. Weber	Consular agent.
Bangkok, Siam	J. M. Hood	Consul.
Do	N. A. McDonald	Vice-consul.
Do	Austin J. Mattingly	Marshal.
Do	N. A. McDonald	Interpreter.
Baracoa, Cuba	P. E. Alayo	Consular agent.
Barbadoes	Jos. G. Morton	Consul.
Do	D. C. DaCosta	Vice-consul.
Barcelona, Spain	J. A. Little	Consul.
Do	Manuel Casajemas	Vice-consul.
Do. Venezuela	H. Baiz	Do.
Barmen, Prussia	J. H. Albers	Consular agent.
Barrington, Nova Scotia	G. Robertson	Do.
Basle, Switzerland	A. L. Wolf	Consul.
Bassein, India	J. Henderson	Consular agent.
Basse Terra, Guadaloupe	A. Lacour	Do.
Batavia, Java	S. Higginson, jr	Consul.
Do		Vice-consul.
Bathurst, West Coast of Africa	Thos. Brown	Consul.
Do	David W. E. Brown	Vice-consul.
Bay of Islands, New Zealand	W. G. Wright	Commercial agent.

LIST OF MINISTERS, CONSULS, ETC.

Consular offices.	Consular officers.	Rank.
Bayonne, France	Gersam Leon	Consular agent.
Beaumaris, Wales	Robt. R. Jones	Do.
Bedeque, Prince Edward Island	J. C. Pope	Do.
Beirut, Syria	J. A. Johnson	Consul general.
Do	H. E. Thompson	Vice-consul general.
Belem, Portugal	T. M. Besoney	Consular clerk.
Belfast, Ireland	Thos. K. King	Consul.
Do	Hugh Creighton	Vice-consul.
Belize, Honduras		Commercial agent.
Do	A. C. Prindle	Vice-commercial agent.
Belleville, Canada	J. W. Carman	Consular agent.
Bergen, Norway	H. J. Lockwood	Consul.
Do		Vice-consul.
Berlin, Prussia	H. Kreismann	Consul.
Bermuda, West Indies	C. M. Allen	Do.
Do	C. F. Allen	Vice-consul.
Bilbao, Spain	Lorenzo Dahl	Consul.
Do	Ed. Aznar	Vice-consul.
Birmingham	Elihu Burritt	Consular agent.
Bissao, Africa		Consul.
Black River, Jamaica	J. W. Leyden	Consular agent.
Bogota, United States of Colombia	G. C. Crane	Consul.
Do		Vice-consul.
Bombay, Bengal	G. A. Kittredge	Consul.
Bonaire, West Indies	W. E. Boye	Consular agent.

LIST OF MINISTERS, CONSULS, ETC.

Consular offices.	Consular officers.	Rank.
Bordeaux, France	W. E. Gleeson	Consul.
Do	Victor Olgioti	Vice-consul.
Bornholm, Denmark	T. H. Ronne	Consular agent.
Boulogne, France	J. de la Montagnie	Consul.
Do	Jos. Fontaine	Vice-consul.
Bradford, England	Geo. M. Towle	Commercial agent.
Do	J. L. Raymond	Vice-commercial agent.
Brake, Oldenburg	B. Muller	Consular agent.
Brantford, Canada	G. C. Baker	Do.
Brava, Verde Islands	J. J. Nunes	Do.
Bremen, Germany	Geo. S. Dodge	Consul.
Do	C. Boernstein	Deputy consul.
Bremerhaven, Germany	F. W. Specht	Consular agent.
Brest, France	J. M. Kerros	Do.
Brindisi, Italy	F. B. Huchting	Consul.
Do	Theo. Titi	Vice-consul.
Brunn, Austria, (Moravia)	G. Schoeller	Consular agent.
Bristol, England	Z. Eastman	Consul.
Do	G. Whitewell	Vice-consul.
Brunai, Borneo		Consul.
Do	J. W. Hoes	Vice-consul.
Brunswick, Germany	W. W. Murphy	Consul.
Do	E. Breuil	Vice-consul.
Brussels, Belgium		Consul.
Do	Aaron Goodrich	Vice-consul.

LIST OF MINISTERS, CONSULS, ETC.

49

Consular offices.	Consular officers.	Rank.
Bucharest, Turkey	L. J. Czapkay	Consul.
Buenaventura, United States of Colombia	J. M. Eder	Do.
Buenos Ayres, Argentine Republic	M. E. Hollister	Do.
Do	F. A. Hollister	Deputy Consul.
Brixham, England	E. Vittery	Consular agent.
Cacilhas, Portugal	D. Affonço	Do.
Cadiz, Spain	R. F. Farrell	Consul.
Do		Vice-consul.
Cagliari, Italy	E. Pernis	Consular agent.
Caipha, Syria	J. Nasrallah	Do.
Cairo, Egypt	G. C. Taylor	Consul.
Do	Felix Walmass	Vice-consul.
Calais, France	J. P. Vendroux	Consular agent.
Calamar, United States of Colombia	J. D. Sanchez	Do.
Calcutta, Bengal	N. P. Jacobs	Consul general.
Do	Chas. H. Bailey	Temporary Vice-consul general.
Caldera, Chili	A. Seiwertz	Consular agent.
Callao, Peru	J. H. McColley	Consul.
Caminha, Portugal	A. M. Rua	Consular agent.
Campeachy, Mexico		Consul.
Canea, Island of Crete, Turkey	W. J. Stillman	Do.
Do	E. A. Alexis	Vice-consul.
Canton, China	Edward M. King	Consul.
Do	C. F. Preston	Interpreter.
Cape Charles & Chateau Bay, Labrador	J. W. Dodge	Consular agent.

7

50 LIST OF MINISTERS, CONSULS, ETC.

Consular offices.	Consular officers.	Rank.
Cape Haytien, Hayti	A. Folsom	Consul.
Cape Town, Cape of Good Hope	Geo. Gerard	Do.
Carácas, Venezuela	E. C. Pruyn	Commercial agent.
Cardenas, Cuba	N. Cross	Consular agent.
Cardiff, Wales	C. E. Burch	Consul.
Carlisle, England	Ed. G. Castle	Commercial agent.
Carlsruhe, Baden	G. F. Kettell	Consul.
Carrara, Italy	F. Torry	Do.
Do	C. Pollina	Vice-consul.
Carthagena, Spain	C. Molina	Consul.
Carthagena, United States of Colombia.	A. S. Hanabergh	Do.
Cascumpec, Prince Edward Island		Consular agent.
Catania, Sicily	A. Peratoner	Do.
Cayenne, Guiana		Consul.
Do		Vice-consul.
Ceara, Brazil	J. S. de Vasconcelles	Consular agent.
Cecimbra, Portugal	F. J. Lopez	Do.
Cette, France	L. S. Nahmens	Do.
Ceylon, India	G. W. Prescott	Commercial agent.
Chatham and Newcastle, N. B	Robert R. Call	Consular agent.
Che Foo, China	E. T. Sandford	Consul.
Chemnitz, Saxony	Henry B. Ryder	Do.
Cherbourg, France	E. Liais	Consular agent.
Chicoutimi, Canada		Do.
Chihuahua, Mexico	C. Moye	Consul.

LIST OF MINISTERS, CONSULS, ETC. 51

Consular offices.	Consular officers.	Rank.
Chihuahua, Mexico		Vice-consul.
Chin Kiang, China	J. L. Kiernan	Consul.
Do.	Chas. J. Sands	Vice-consul.
Chittagong, India	W. Farlie	Consular agent.
Christiansand, Norway	O. C. Reinhardt	Do.
Cienfuegos, Cuba	Chas. Fox	Do.
Ciudad Bolivar, Venezuela	John Dalton	Consul.
Do		Vice-consul.
Civita Vecchia, Italy	G. Marsanick	Consular agent.
Clifton, Canada	W. Martin Jones	Consul.
Do		Vice-consul.
Coaticook, Canada	C. H. Powers	Consul.
Do	Thos. B. Trihey	Vice-consul.
Do	Alden E. Martin	Deputy consul.
Cobija, Bolivia	C. Milne	Consul.
Cobourg, Canada	E. S. Winans	Consular agent.
Cognac, France	A. Matuspi	Do.
Cologne, Prussia	G. Holscher	Do.
Colombo, Ceylon	R. Dawson	Vice-commercial agent.
Comayagua and Tegucigalpa, Honduras	W. C. Burchard	Consul.
Concelho da Boncas, Portugal	A. F. A. Guimaraes	Consular agent.
Constantinople, Turkey	J. H. Goodenow	Consul general.
Do	Jos. Garguilo	Vice-consul general.
Do	A. Thompson	Marshal.
Do	J. Garguilo	Acting deputy marshal.

52 LIST OF MINISTERS, CONSULS. ETC.

Consular offices.	Consular officers.	Rank.
Copenhagen, Denmark		Consul.
Do	L. A. Hecksher	Vice-consul.
Coquimbo, Chili	C. C. Greene	Consul.
Do	J. Jenkins	Deputy consul.
Corfu, Ionian Isles	T. Woodley	Consular agent.
Cork, Ireland	E. G. Eastman	Consul.
Corunna, Spain	A. G. Fuertes	Consular agent.
Cow Bay, Nova Scotia	C. Archibald	Do.
Cowes, England	T. Harling	Do.
Crefeld, Prussia	Julius Magnus	Do.
Cronstadt, Russia	A. Wilkins	Do.
Crookhaven, Ireland		Do.
Cumaña, Venezuela	W. S. Cunningham	Do.
Curaçon, West Indies	James Faxon	Consul.
Do	W. V. E. Horan	Vice-consul.
Cyprus, Turkey	L. P. di Cesnola	Consul.
Damascus, Syria	M. Meshaka	Consular agent.
Dantzig, Prussia	P. Collas	Do.
Dardanelles, Turkey	C. Calvert	Do.
Dartmouth, England	R. Kingston	Do.
Demerara, British Guiana	P. Figyelmesy	Consul.
Do	A. Duff	Vice-consul.
Denia, Spain	J. Morand	Consul.
Dieppe, France	J. Le Vert	Consular agent.
Digby, Nova Scotia	J. C. Wade	Do.

LIST OF MINISTERS, CONSULS, ETC.

53

Consular offices.	Consular officers.	Rank.
Dresden, Saxony	W. S. Campbell	Consul.
Drontheim, Norway	J. F. Finne	Consular agent.
Dublin, Ireland	W. B. West	Consul.
Do	Jno. Rainsford	Vice-consul.
Dundalk, Ireland		Consular agent.
Dundee, Scotland	J. Smith	Consul.
Dundee, Canada	J. McMillen	Consular agent.
Dunedin, N. Z.	H. Driver	Do.
Dunkirk, France	Henri Lematlre	Do.
Dunmore Town, Bahama	Wm. H. Sears	Do.
Dunville, Canada		Do.
Dusseldorf, Prussia	Henry Louis	Do.
East Harbor, Turk's Island	E. Jones	Do.
Elsinore, Denmark	G. P. Hansen	Consul.
Espinho, Portugal	J. J. D'Almeida	Consular agent.
Falmouth, England	A. Fox	Consul.
Do	H. Fox	Deputy consul.
Falmouth, Jamaica	R. Nunes	Consular agent.
Fano, Denmark	J. K. Bork	Do.
Faro, Portugal	F. L. Javarez	Do.
Fayal, Azores	C. W. Dabney	Consul.
Do	J. P. Dabney	Deputy consul.
Do	Sam'l W. Dabney	Do.
Figueira, Portugal	C. Laidley	Consular agent.
Fiume, Austria	L. Francovitch	Do.

54 LIST OF MINISTERS, CONSULS, ETC.

Consular offices.	Consular officers.	Rank.
Florence, Italy	T. B. Lawrence	Consul general.
Do	J. C. Matteini	Vice-consul general.
Do		Consular clerk.
Flores, Azores	F. J. M. Henriques	Consular agent.
Fogo, Cape Verde Islands	J. C. Bubosa	Do.
Foo-Chow, China	Alfred Allen	Consul.
Do	Thos. Dunn	Vice-consul.
Do	B. S. Lyman	Marshal.
Fort de France, Martinique	A. Nollet	Consular agent.
Fort Erie, Canada	F. N. Blake	Consul.
Frankfort-on-the-Main, Prussia	W. W. Murphy	Consul general.
Do	Chas. Graebe	Vice-consul general.
Do	Aug. Glaser	Consular clerk.
Fredericton, N. B.	S. Barker	Consular agent.
Frederickshaven, Denmark	P. C. Kall	Do.
Frederickstadt, Santa Cruz	W. F. Moore	Do.
Freemantle, Australia	T. Pope	Do.
Freeligsburg, Canada	Gaius M. Blodgett	Do.
Funchal, Madeira	Chas. A. Leas	Consul.
Gaboon, Africa	Aug. Perrot	Commercial agent.
Do	Ira M. Preston	Vice-commercial agent.
Galatza, Moldavia	A. Hartmann	Consul.
Do	Emil Hartmann	Vice-consul.
Gallipoli, Italy	C. Clauson	Consular agent.
Galway, Ireland	W. B. West	Consul.

LIST OF MINISTERS, CONSULS, ETC.

55

Consular offices.	Consular officers.	Rank.
Gananoque	E. E. Abbot	Consular agent.
Gaspé Basin, Canada	H. Le Bontillier	Consul.
Do		Vice-consul.
Geestemunde, Prussia	W. Colvin Brown	Consul.
Gefle, Sweden	R. Rettig	Consular agent.
Geneva, Switzerland	C. H. Upton	Consul.
Genoa, Italy	O. M. Spencer	Do.
Do	Joseph Valerio	Vice-consul.
Georgetown, P. E. Island	A. A. McDonald	Consular agent.
Ghent, Belgium		Consul.
Do	D. Levison	Vice-consul.
Gibara, Cuba	E. R. Codrington	Consular agent.
Gibraltar, Spain	H. J. Sprague	Consul.
Girgenti, Italy	L. Granet	Consular agent.
Glasgow, Scotland	Wm. L. Duff	Consul.
Do	Wm. Cook	Vice-consul.
Gloucester, England	E. L. Kendall	Consular agent.
Gluckstadt, Denmark	J. S. Schenck	Do.
Goderich, Canada	Thos. Allcock	Consul.
Gonaives, Hayti	A. Hilchenback	Consular agent.
Gottenburg, Sweden	F. K. Bazier	Consul.
Do		Vice-consul.
Graciosa, Azores	B. A. da C. S. Bettencourtt.	Consular agent.
Grand Bassa, Liberia	L. F. Richardson	Commercial agent.
Grand Caymans, Jamaica	W. Eden	Consular agent.

56   LIST OF MINISTERS, CONSULS, ETC.

Consular offices.	Consular officers.	Rank.
Green Turtle Bay, West Indies	Uriah Saunders	Consular agent.
Guadaloupe, West Indies	H. Thionville	Consul.
Guanatañamo, Cuba	F. Badell	Consular agent.
Guatemala, (city)	E. Uhl	Consul.
Guayama, Porto Rico	E. M. Verges	Consular agent.
Guayanilla, Porto Rico		Do.
Guayaquil, Ecuador	E. Lee	Consul.
Guaymas, Mexico	A. Willard	Do.
Do	J. P. Winegar	Vice-consul.
Guernsey, Great Britain	A. Carey	Consular agent.
Guysborough, Nova Scotia	C. H. Franchville	Do.
Hakodadi, Japan	E. E. Rice	Consul.
Do	N. Emery Rice	Vice-consul.
Halifax, Nova Scotia	M. M. Jackson	Consul.
Do	N. Gunnison	Vice-consul.
Hamberg, Germany	S. T. Williams	Consul.
Do	Jas. R. McDonald	Vice-consul.
Hamilton, Bermuda	J. T. Darrell	Consular agent.
Hamilton, Canada	Daniel R. Boice	Consul.
Hankow, China	G. H. C. Salter	Do.
Do		Vice-consul.
Do		Marshal.
Hammerfest, Norway		Consular agent.
Harbor Grace, N. F.	Chas. Wills	Do.
Havana, Cuba	Alvin Hawkins	Consul general.

LIST OF MINISTERS, CONSULS, ETC. 57

Consular offices.	Consular officers.	Rank.
Havana, Cuba	H. R. de La Reintrie	Vice-consul general.
Do	John M. Utley	Consular clerk.
Harburg	J. D. Westedt	Consular agent.
Havre, France	Dwight Morris	Consul.
Do	J. Hunt	Vice-consul.
Helsingfors, Finland	R. Frenckell	Do.
Hemmingford, Canada	G. W. Burdick	Consular agent.
Hesse Cassel, Prussia	W. W. Murphy	Consul.
Hesse Darmstadt	W. W. Murphy	Do.
Hesse Hombourg, Prussia	W. W. Murphy	Do.
Hilo, Hawaiian Islands		Do.
Do	J. Worth	Vice-consul.
Hobart Town, Tasmania	D. McPherson, jr	Consul.
Honfleur, France	C. Wagner	Consular agent.
Hong Kong, China	Isaac J. Allen	Consul.
Honolulu, Hawaiian Islands	Z. S. Spalding	Do.
Do		Vice-consul.
Huddersfield, England	Geo. P. Kebler	Consular agent.
Huelva, Spain	M. Zafra	Do.
Hull, England	H. J. Atkinson	Do.
Huntingdon, Canada		Do.
Iloilo, Philippine Islands	W. B. Loring	Do.
Inagua, Bahamas	D. Sargent	Do.
Isle de Re, France	E. L. Roullet	Do.
Ivica, (Island)	Wm. Wallis	Do.

8

58   LIST OF MINISTERS, CONSULS, ETC.

Consular offices.	Consular officers.	Rank.
Jacmel, Hayti	Charles Moravia	Agent of comm'l agent
Jaffa, Turkey	T. F. H. Svarenthal	Consular agent.
Jalapa, Mexico	C. L. Kennedy	Do.
Jeremie, Hayti	J. Vigoureux	Agent of comm'l agent
Jersey Island	T. Renouf	Consular agent.
Jerusalem, Syria	V. Beauboucher	Consul.
Do	L. M. Johnson	Vice-consul.
Do	L. M. Johnson	Consular clerk.
Do	B. Finkelstein	Deputy consul.
Kanagawa, Japan	Julius Stahel	Consul.
Do	Paul Frank	Marshal.
Do	T. A. H. Schepel	Interpreter.
Kingston, Jamaica	Aaron Gregg	Consul.
Do	J. N. Camp	Vice-consul.
Kingston, Canada	S. B. Hance	Consul.
Kingstown, Ireland		Consular agent.
Kiu Kiang, China	S. S. Gilbert	Do.
Konigsburg, Prussia	J. H. Brockman	Consular agent.
Kurrachee, Sinde	B. F. Farnham	Do.
Lachine, Canada	Wm. H. Calvert	Do.
Lacolle, Canada		Do.
Lagos, Portugal	J. M. Mascarenhas	Do.
Laguayra, Venezuela	C. H. Loehr	Consul.
Laguna, Mexico		Do.
Do	M. R. Carballo	Vice-consul.

LIST OF MINISTERS, CONSULS, ETC.

59

Consular offices.	Consular officers.	Rank.
Lahaina, Hawaiian Islands	E. Perkins	Consul.
Do	E. P. Adams	Vice-consul.
Lambayeque, Peru	S. C. Montjoy	Consul.
Do		Vice-consul.
Lanthala, Feejee Islands	J. M. Brower	Commercial agent.
Lanzarotte, Canary Islands	J. T. Topham	Consular agent.
La Paz, San José, and Cape St. Lucas, Mexico	Francis B. Elmer	Consul.
Do	C. A. Parsons	Vice-consul.
Las Palmas, Canary Islands	F. W. Manly	Consular agent.
La Tremblade, France	M. Robineau	Do.
La Rochelle, France	Thomas P. Smith	Consul.
Latakia, Syria	S. Vitali	Consular agent.
La Union, San Salvador	J. F. Flint	Consul.
Do		Vice-consul.
Leca, Portugal	J. da C. T. Guimaraes	Consular agent.
Leeds, England		Consul.
Do	Clark Smith	Vice-consul.
Leghorn, Italy	J. Hutchinson	Consul.
Leith, Scotland	John S. Fiske	Do.
Do	Jas. Galloway	Vice-consul.
Leipsic, Saxony	M. J. Cramer	Consul.
Do	Thos. McGee	Vice-consul.
Licata, Italy	Ludovico Saito	Consular agent.
Liege, Belgium	Arthur Genaert	Consul.

LIST OF MINISTERS, CONSULS, ETC.

Consular offices.	Consular officers.	Rank.
Leige, Belgium		Vice-consul.
Limerick, Ireland	M. R. Ryan	Consular agent.
Limoges, France		Do.
Lingan, Nova Scotia	F. E. Leaver	Do.
Lisbon, Portugal	C. A. Munro	Consul.
Do	C. F. J. Hutchens	Vice-consul.
Liverpool, England	T. H. Dudley	Consul.
Do	H. Wilding	Vice-consul.
Do	L. W. Viollier	Consular clerk.
Liverpool, Nova Scotia		Consular agent.
Llanelly, Wales	R. Dunkin	Consular agent.
London, England	F. H. Morse	Consul.
Do	J. Nunn	Deputy consul.
Londonderry, Ireland	A. Henderson	Consul.
L'Orient, France		Consular agent.
Lota and Coronel, Chile	James Silvey	Do.
Lyons, France	P. J. Osterhaus	Consul.
Do	Albert J. de Zeyk	Deputy consul.
Do	Albert J. de Zeyk	Consular clerk.
Lubec, Germany	W. W. Murphy	Consul.
Do	Wm. Coleman	Vice-consul.
Ludwigshafen, Baden	S. Sederle	Consular agent.
Macao, China		Consul.
Do	Henerich Ebell	Vice consul.
Maceio, Brazil	J. Borstelmann	Consular agent.

LIST OF MINISTERS, CONSULS, ETC.

61

Consular offices.	Consular officers.	Rank.
Madras. British India		Consular agent.
Maio, Cape Verde Islands	J. H. Evora	Do.
Malaga, Spain	A. M. Hancock	Consul.
Do	J. R. Geary	Vice-consul.
Malta, (Island)	W. Winthrop	Consul.
Manchester, England	H. G. Wells	Do.
Manila, Phillippine Islands	J. B. Pierson	Do.
Do	J. Russell	Vice-consul.
Manheim, Baden	L. Stoll	Consular agent.
Manzanillo, Cuba	M. R. Ecay	Do.
Manzanillo, Mexico	J. H. Noteware	Consul.
Maracaibo, Venezuela	E. Sturmfels	Do.
Do	F. C. Jutting	Acting vice-consul.
Maranham, Brazil	W. H. Evans	Consul.
Marsala, Italy	R. L. Hervey	Consular agent.
Marseilles, France	M. F. Conway	Consul.
Do	Fred. W. Achille	Vice-consul.
Matamoras, Mexico	J. White	Consul.
Do	L. Avery	Vice-consul.
Matanzas, Cuba	H. C. Hall	Consul.
Maulmain, India	W. Brooke	Consular agent.
Mayaguez, Porto Rico	J. C. Coxe	Do.
Mazatlan, Mexico	I. Sisson	Commercial agent.
Medellin, United States of Colombia		Do.
Media, Tunisia	J. Lombroso	Consular agent.

62 LIST OF MINISTERS, CONSULS, ETC.

Consular offices.	Consular officers.	Rank.
Melbourne, Australia	Geo. R. Latham	Consul.
Memel, Prussia	H. Fowler	Consular agent.
Mentone, France	N. Viale	Do.
Merida and Sisal, Mexico	R. J. y Patrullo	Consul.
Messina, Italy	F. W. Behn	Do.
Do.		Vice-consul.
Mexico, (city)	John Black	Do.
Mier, Mexico	W. G. Jones	Consular agent.
Milan, Italy	W. Clark	Do.
Milford Haven, Wales	A. B. Harries	Do.
Minatitlan, Mexico	R. C. M. Hoyt	Consul.
Morales, Mexico		Commercial agent.
Monganui, New Zealand	C. W. Drury	Consular agent.
Monrovia, Africa	John Seys	Min. Res. & Con. Gen'l.
Montego Bay, Jamaica	G. L. Phillips	Consular agent.
Montevideo, Uruguay	J. D. Long	Consul.
Monterey, Mexico	J. Ulrich	Do.
Montreal, Canada	Wm. W. Averell	Consul general.
Do.	Thos. F. Wilson	Vice-consul general.
Do.	Thos. F. Wilson	Consular clerk.
Morlaix, France	M. Alexandre	Consular agent.
Morpeth, Canada		Do.
Moscow, Russia	Eugene Schuyler	Consul.
Do.	Samuel P. Young	Vice-consul.
Mossel Bay, Cape Town, Africa	E. Eager	Consular agent.

LIST OF MINISTERS, CONSULS, ETC.

Consular offices.	Consular officers.	Rank.
Mozambique, Africa	Caleb Cooke..............	Consul.
Mulhouse, France......	August Strohl...........	Consular agent.
Munich, Bavaria	Henry Toomy	Consul.
Nagasaki, Japan	W. P. Mangum...........	Do.
Do............................	D. L. Moore	Vice-consul.
Naguabo, Porto Rico................	W. Haddock.............	Consular agent.
Napanee, Canada West	Hugh Ralston	Do.
Nantes, France......................	Benj. Gerrish, jr........	Consul.
Do...........................	J. Dedichen	Vice-consul.
Naples, Italy........................	Rob't L. Matthews	Consul.
Do..........................	Rob't Rogers	Vice-consul.
Napoleon Vendée, France	J. W. McClure	Consul.
Nassau, Europe......................	W. W. Murphy	Do.
Nassau, West Indies................	T. Kirkpatrick...........	Do.
Nee-e-gata, Japan....................	....	Consular agent.
Newcastle-upon-Tyne, England.......	J. H. McChesney	Consul.
Do	T. P. Orwin	Vice-consul.
Newcastle, New South Wales..........	G. Mitchell..............	Consular agent.
New Chwang, China	F. P. Knight	Consul.
Do	....	Vice-consul.
Newport, England	J. N. Knapp.............	Consular agent.
Nice, France	A. O. Aldis.............	Consul.
Do	Chas. Luigi	Vice-consul.
Ningpo, China......................	E. C. Lord..............	Consul.
Nottingham, England	F. G. Rawson	Consular agent.

64 LIST OF MINISTERS, CONSULS, ETC.

Consular offices.	Consular officers.	Rank.
Nuremburg, Bavaria	Benj. Le Fevre	Consul.
Nuevitas, Cuba	R. Gibbs	Consular agent.
Odessa, Russia	T. C. Smith	Consul.
Oldenburg, Germany	H. W. Carstens	Do.
Old Harbor, Ja	Moses Bravo	Consular agent.
Old Hartlepool, England	C. Nielson	Do.
Olten, Switzerland	H. Salathe	Do.
Omoa and Truxillo, Honduras	C. R. Follin	Consul.
Oporto, Portugal	H. W. Diman	Do.
Do	M. R. Jones	Vice-consul.
Oran, Africa	Antonin Sarrat	Consular agent.
Osacca and Hiogo, Japan	T. Scott Stewart	Consul.
Ostend, Belgium	A. Van Iseghem Duclos	Do.
Otranto, Italy	Wm. M. Mayo	Do.
Ottawa, Canada West	P. H. Mehar	Consular agent.
Ovar, Portugal	J. A. D'Almeida	Do.
Paco d'Arcos, Portugal	F. F. Godinho	Do.
Padang, Sumatra		Consul.
Do	A. Van Gils	Vice-consul.
Palermo, Italy	L. Monti	Consul.
Palma, Canary Islands	F. P. Laremuth	Consular agent.
Palma, Majorca	J. Fiol	Do.
Panama, United States of Colombia	T. K. Smith	Consul.
Do	J. Hough	Vice-consul.
Para, Brazil	J. B. Bond	Consul.

LIST OF MINISTERS, CONSULS, ETC.

Consular offices.	Consular officers.	Rank.
Paraiba, Brazil		Consular agent.
Paramaribo, Dutch Guiana	H. Sawyer	Consul.
Paris, France	John G. Nicolay	Do.
Do	Franklin Olcott	Vice-consul.
Do	James Hand	Consular clerk.
Do	Wm. Heine	Do.
Do	Franklin Olcott	Do.
Parnahiba, Brazil	E. Burnett	Commercial agent.
Paso del Norte, Mexico		Consul.
Do	Wm. F. Hellen	Vice-consul.
Pau, France	G. de M. Clay	Consular agent.
Patras, Greece	F. Fachiri	Do.
Payta, Peru	R. M. Columbus	Consul.
Do	I. L. Havens	Vice-consul.
Pelotas, Brazil	B. R. Cordeiro	Consular agent.
Penang, East Indies		Do.
Pernambuco, Brazil	T. Adamson, jr	Consul.
Do	W. H. McGrath	Vice-consul.
Peso de Regra, Portugal		Consular agent.
Pesth, Hungary	Adolf Klein	Do.
Pictou, Nova Scotia	B. H. Norton	Consul.
Picton, Canada	Robt. Clapp	Consular agent.
Piedras Negras, Mexico	W. Schuchardt	Commercial agent.
Piræus, Greece	Matthew Megis	Consul.
Do	Jonas King	Vice-consul.

9

66 LIST OF MINISTERS, CONSULS, ETC.

Consular offices.	Consular officers.	Rank.
Plymouth, England	T. W. Fox	Consul.
Do	H. Fox	Deputy consul.
Ponce, Porto Rico	Peter Minvielle	Consular agent.
Porsgrund, Norway	Carl J. Kraby	Consul.
Portsmouth, England	Geo. Baker	Consular agent.
Porto Alegre, Brazil	F. J. Monteiro	Do.
Port Baltic, Prussia	C. Kalk	Do.
Port Bruce, Canada		Do.
Port Burwell, Canada		Do.
Port Colbourne, Canada		Do.
Port Dover, Canada		Do.
Port Elizabeth, Cape Colony, Africa	J. L. Flanders	Do.
Port Hope, Canada	Thos. P. Jones	Do.
Port Louis, Mauritius	Nicholas Pike	Consul.
Do	F. O. Robinson	Vice-consul.
Port Mahon, Minorca	H. B. Robinson	Consul.
Port Natal, Africa	G. C. Cato	Consular agent.
Port au Prince, Hayti		Min. res. and con. gen'l.
Do	H. Conard	Vice-commercial agent.
Port Orotava, Teneriffe		Consular agent.
Port Rowan, Canada	Geo. C. Baker	Do.
Port Sarnia, Canada	Andrew W. Duggan	Consul.
Do	A. Hendricks	Vice-consul.
Port Stanley, Canada	Chas. Morrill	Consular agent.
Port Stanley, Falkland Islands		Commercial agent.

LIST OF MINISTERS, CONSULS, ETC.

67

Consular offices.	Consular officers.	Rank.
Port Stanley, Falkland Islands.......	Geo. M. Dean	Vice-commercial agent.
Port St. Mary, Spain	E. Crusoe..............	Consular agent.
Port of Sidney, Cape Breton	J. P. Ward	Do.
Porto Plata, Hayti	F. J. Waldmayer	Agent of comm'l agent.
Prague, Bohemia....................	J. Von Geitler...........	Consular agent.
Prescott, Canada....................	James Weldon...........	Consul.
Prince Edward Island..............	E. Parker Scammon......	Do.
Puerto Cabello, Venezuela............	A. Lacombe	Do.
Do....	....	Vice-consul.
Puerto Plata, St. Domingo	Wm. Lithgow	Ac't vice-comm'l agent.
Pugwash, Nova Scotia..............	H. G. Pineo............	Consular agent.
Punta Arenas, Costa Rica............	W. Dent...............	Do.
Punta Arenas, Nicaragua.............	B. S. Cotrell............	Commercial agent.
Quebec, Canada	Chas Robinson..........	Consul.
Do.........	Geo. H. Holt	Vice-consul.
Queensland, Australia	J. E. Brown	Consular agent.
Quibdo, U. S. of Colombia...........	G. P. Gamba	Consul.
Ragged Islands	....	Consular agent.
Ramleh, Syria	H. Nunkos	Do.
Rangoon, Burmah...................	G. Bullock	Do.
Ravenna, Italy.....................	John Reichard..........	Consul.
Redonda, W. I.....................	Ed. H. Mau	Ac't vice-comm'l agent.
Regoa, Portugal	F. da C. Guilherme	Consular agent.
Retimo, Isle of Crete	G. Lariacki	Do.
Revel, Russia......................	H. B. Stacy	Consul.

68 LIST OF MINISTERS, CONSULS, ETC.

Consular offices.	Consular officers.	Rank.
Revel, Russia	W. Mayer	Vice-consul.
Reims, France	A G. Gill	Consul.
Rhenish Bavaria	G. F. Kettell	Do.
Riga, Russia	A. Schwartz	Do.
Ringkjobing, Denmark	A. C. Hustedt	Consular agent.
Rio de Janeiro, Brazil	J. Monroe	Consul.
Do	H. E. Milford	Vice-consul.
Rio Grande, Brazil	A. Young, jr	Consul.
Rio Hacha, United States of Colombia	N. Danies	Do.
Do	M. Meyer	Vice-consul.
Rio Negro, Argentine Confederation		Consul.
Ritzebüttel and Cuxhaven, Germany	G. von der Meden	Consular agent.
Rochefort, France	A. G. Brellonin	Do.
Rome, Italy	E. C. Cushman	Consul.
Do	H. B. Brown	Vice-consul.
Ronne, Denmark	T. H. Ronne	Consular agent.
Roseau, Dominica	Victor Blanchard	Commercial agent.
Rosario, Argentine Confederation	W. Wheelwright	Do.
Do		Vice-commercial agent.
Rotterdam, Netherlands	Albert Rhodes	Consul.
Do	A. A. Wambersie	Vice-consul.
Rouen, France	Louis Guebert	Consular agent.
Sabanilla, United States of Colombia	E. P. Pellet	Commercial agent.
Sable d'Olonnes, France		Consular agent.
Sado, Japan		Do.

LIST OF MINISTERS, CONSULS, ETC.

69

Consular offices.	Consular officers.	Rank.
Sagua la Grande, Cuba	J. H. Horner	Consular agent.
Sal, Cape Verde Islands	J. J. Vera Cruz	Do.
Salt Cay, Turk's Islands	W. H. Harrott	Do.
Saltillo, Mexico	J. H. Porter	Consular agent.
San Andrés, Caribbean Sea	P. B. Livingston	Vice-commercial agent.
San Blas, Mexico	D. Fergusson	Commercial agent.
San José, Costa Rica		Do.
San José do Norte, Brazil	C. M. V. Araujo	Consular agent.
San José, Mexico	E. Jallespie	Do.
San José and Pimental, Peru	W. V. Fry	Do.
San José de Guatemala	G. F. Willemsen	Vice-consul.
San Juan de los Remedios	I. Stone	Do.
San Juan del Norte, Nicaragua	B. S. Cotrell	Commercial agent.
San Juan del Sur, Nicaragua	R. Mead	Consul.
Do	A. L. Tompkins	Vice-consul.
San Juan, Porto Rico	A. Jourdan	Consul.
Do	C. A. Hoard	Vice-consul.
San Luis Potosi, Mexico		Consul.
Do	J. A. Piernas	Vice-consul.
San Salvador, (city)	E. A. Wright	Consul.
Santa Cruz, Cuba	Chas. Hugar	Consular agent.
Santa Cruz, West Indies	E. H. Perkins	Consul.
Do	Robt. A. Finley	Vice-consul.
Santa Martha, U. States of Colombia	F. D. Garcia	Commercial agent.
Santa Rosa, Mexico	Charles Schurchard	Consular agent.

LIST OF MINISTERS, CONSULS, ETC.

Consular offices.	Consular officers.	Rank.
Santander, Spain	Louis Gallo	Consul.
Santander, Spain		Vice-consul.
Santiago, Cape Verde Islands	Benj. Tripp, jr	Consul.
Santiago de Cuba	E. F. Wallace	Do.
Do	J. Badell	Vice-consul.
Santos, Brazil	C. F. de Vivaldi	Consul.
Do	E. L. Meade	Vice-consul.
Savanna la Mar, Jamaica	James Dougall	Consular agent.
Scheidam, Netherlands	P. Prius	Do.
Schwerin, Germany	Orrin J. Rose	Consul.
Scilly, (Island.)	T. J. Bruxton	Consular agent.
Scio, Turkey	N. Pelrocochino	Consul.
Do		Vice-consul.
Sedan, France		Consular agent.
Seville, Spain	J. Cunningham	Consul.
Setubal, Portugal	C. F. O'Neil	Consular agent.
Seychelles, Indian Ocean	Dorence Atwater	Consul.
Shanghai, China	G. F. Seward	Consul general.
Do	W. P. Mangum	Vice-consul general.
Do		Marshal.
Do	B. Jenkins	Interpreter.
Do	Burge R. Lewis	Consular clerk.
Do	O. B. Bradford	Do.
Sheffield, England	George J. Abbot	Consul.
Do	Chas. A. Branson	Vice-consul.

LIST OF MINISTERS, CONSULS, ETC.

71

Consular offices.	Consular officers.	Rank.
Shelburne, Nova Scotia		Consular agent.
Sidon, Syria	S. Abela	Do.
Sierra Leone, Africa	H. Rider	Commercial agent.
Do	T. Rosenbush	Vice-commercial agent.
Simonstown, Africa	Patrick D. Martin	Consular agent.
Sines, Portugal	J. P. de M. Falcao	Do.
Singapore, India	I. Stone	Consul.
Do	Wm. B. Smith	Vice-consul.
Smyrna, Turkey	Enoch J. Smithers	Consul.
Do	J. Griffit	Vice-consul.
Sonneberg, Germany	S. Hirshbach	Consul.
Sonsonate, Salvador	I. Mathé	Do.
Sourabaya, Java	C. von Oven	Consular agent.
Souris, Prince Edward Island	J. Night	Do.
Southampton, England	J. Britton	Consul.
Spezia, Italy	W. T. Rice	Do.
St. Ann's Bay, Ja	M. Solomons	Consular agent.
St. Andrew, New Brunswick	Ed. Dorimer	Do.
St. Bartholomew, West Indies	R. Burton Dinzey	Commercial agent.
St. Catharine's, Canada	D. C. Haynes	Consular agent.
St. Catherine's Island, Brazil	B. Lindsey	Consul.
St. Christopher, West Indies	E. S. Delisle	Commercial agent.
St. Domingo, (city)	J. S. Smith	Do.
St. Etienne, France	Geo. Bechtel	Consular agent.
St. Gallen, Switzerland	Wm. Auer	Do.

72 LIST OF MINISTERS, CONSULS, ETC.

Consular offices.	Consular officers.	Rank.
St. George, New Brunswick..........	Geo. Baker	Consular agent.
St. Helena, (Island.)................	Thos. Fitnam	Commercial agent.
St. Helens, England.................	J. Hammill	Consular agent.
St. Johns, Canada East..............	Luther P. Blodgett.......	Consul.
St. John's, N. F.	Thos. N. Molloy.........	Do.
Do.... ...., ...	Chas. Wills	Vice-consul.
St. John, N. B......................	D. B. Warner	Consul.
St. Joao da Foz, Portugal............	S. J. Vasconcellos.....,..	Consular agent.
St. Malo, France	....	Do.
St. Manra, Greece...................	A. Slamatopulo	Do.
St. Marc, Hayti.....................	F. W. Clapp	Vice-commercial agent.
St. Martin, West Indies..............	C. Rey	Consul.
St. Michael, Azores.................	T. Hickling	Consular agent.
St. Nazaire, France.................	J. Van Duym............	Do.
St. Paul de Loando, Africa...........	A. A. Silva..............	Commercial agent.
Do.........	F. A. Silva..............	Vice-commercial agent.
St. Pierre, Martinique...............	....	Consul.
Do....................	H. David	Vice-consul.
St. Pierre, Miquelon, ...	J. P. Frecker...........	Commercial agent.
Do......	W. F. McLaughlin.......	Vice-commercial agent.
St. Petersburg, Russia...............	Geo. Pomutz	Consul.
Do......	J. Curtin...............	Vice-consul.
St. Stephen, New Brunswick	G. M. Porter	Consular agent.
St. Thomas, West Indies.............	Jno. T. Robeson	Consul.
Do......	E. B. Simmons	Vice-consul.

LIST OF MINISTERS, CONSULS, ETC.

73

Consular offices.	Consular officers.	Rank.
St. Thomas, Africa	D. L. Marsins	Consul.
St. Thomas, Ontario	Chas. Morrill	Consular agent.
St. Valery, France		Do.
St. Vincent, Cape Verde Islands	Wm. E. Huges	Do.
Stanstead, Canada		Do.
Stavanger, Norway	T. Falk	Do.
Stettin, Prussia	L. R. Roeder	Consul.
Do	A. E. Wendt	Vice-consul.
Stockholm, Sweden		Consul.
Strasbourg, France	Edward Robinson	Do.
Do	T. Krüger	Deputy consul.
Stuttgard, Wurtemburg	E. Klauprecht	Consul.
Sunderland, England	H. Brown	Consular agent.
Sverabaya, Java	Carl von Oven	Do.
Swansea, Wales	H. Morice	Do.
Swatow, China	J. C. A. Wingate	Consul.
Do	C. W. Bradley	Vice-consul.
Do		Marshal.
Swinemünde, Prussia	A. Radman	Consular agent.
Sydney, New South Wales	H. H. Hall	Commercial agent.
Sydney, Cape Breton	T. D. Archibald	Consular agent.
Syra, Greece	E. Sapouzaki	Do.
Syracuse, Sicily	N. Stelle	Do.
Tabasco, Mexico	F. M. de Nemegyei	Commercial agent.
Taganrog, Russia	Antoine Sedemonte	Consular agent.

10

LIST OF MINISTERS, CONSULS, ETC.

Consular offices.	Consular officers.	Rank.
Tahiti, Society Islands	F. A. Perkins	Consul.
Talcahuano, Chili	W. W. Randall	Do.
Do	J. Silvey	Vice-consul.
Tamatave, Madagascar	J. P. Finkelmeir	Commercial agent.
Tampico, Mexico	F. Chase	Consul general.
Tangier, Morocco	J. H. McMath	Consul.
Taranto, Italy		Consul.
Tarragona, Spain	A. Muller	Consular agent.
Tarsus, Asia Minor	A. Debbas	Do.
Tehuantepec, Mexico	C. C. Finkler	Consul.
Teneriffe, Canary Islands	W. H. Dabney	Do.
Do	B. Forstall	Vice-consul.
Terceira, Azores	T. de Castro	Consular agent.
Tetuan, Africa	J. S. Levy	Commercial agent.
Thisted, Denmark	J. Nyeborg	Consular agent.
Tien-Tsin, China		Consul.
Do		Vice-consul.
Toronto, Canada	D. Thurston	Consul.
Toulon, France	P. Andiffret	Consular agent.
Trapani, Sicily	O. Turbino	Do.
Trebisond, Turkey in Asia		Consul.
Trieste, Austria	A. W. Thayer	Do.
Trinidad de Cuba	F. F. Cavada	Do.
Do	A. Von Uslar	Vice-consul.
Trinidad, (Island)	R. P. Harmon	Consul.

LIST OF MINISTERS, CONSULS, ETC.

75

Consular offices.	Consular officers.	Rank.
rinidad, (Island)	Edward H. Fitt.	Vice-consul.
ripoli, **Africa**	W. Porter	Consul.
ripoli, **Syria**	A. Yanuni	Consular agent.
romso, **Norway**		Do.
ruxillo, **Honduras**	E. Prudot	Do.
umaco, U. S. of Colombia	W. H. Wier	Consul.
unis, **Africa**	G. H. Heap	Do.
unstall, England	T. Lewellyn	Consular agent.
urbo, U. S. of Colombia		Consul.
urk's Islands	Oliver Mungen	Do.
Do	J. C. Crisson	Deputy consul.
utuila, Navigator's Islands	J. Schwineke	Vice-commercial agent.
yre, **Syria**	Y. Aknad	Consular agent.
alencia, Spain	Levi H. Coit	Consul.
Do		Vice-consul.
alparaiso, Chili	A. W. Clark	Consul.
Do	J. Silvey	Vice-consul.
elez Malaga, Spain	J. R. Geary	Consular agent.
enice, **Italy**	Francis Colton	Consul.
Do	L. G. Mead, jr	Vice-consul.
era Cruz, Mexico	E. H. Saulnier	Consul.
Do	A. S. Calderon	Vice-consul.
erviers, Belgium		Consul.
ianna, Portugal	J. C. da Silva Lima	Consular agent.

76 LIST OF MINISTERS, CONSULS, ETC.

Consular offices.	Consular officers.	Rank.
Victoria, V. I.	A. Francis	Consul.
Viegue, West Indies	Lane Garben	Consular agent.
Vienna, Austria	P. S. Post	Consul.
Do.	D. F. Koshammer	Vice-consul.
Do.	B. M. Wilson	Consular clerk.
Vigo, Spain	M. Barcena	Consul.
Villa do Conde, Portugal	J. A. de Sousa	Consular agent.
Villa Novo, Portugal	M. de Guedes	Do.
Villa Real de San Antonio, Portugal	M. G. Roldan	Do.
Waterford, Ireland	R. P. Williams	Do.
West Caicos, Turk's Islands	S. Winter	Do.
West Hartlepool, England	C. Nielson	Do.
Weymouth, England	W. Roberts	Do.
Wexford, Ireland	J. W. Walsh	Do.
Whampoa, China	H. N. Blanchard	Do.
Windsor, Nova Scotia	P. S. Burnham	Do.
Windsor, Canada	Andrew J. Stevens	Consul.
Worcester, England	T. Southall	Consular agent.
Wyborg, Finland	J. Sparrow	Do.
Wyk-on-För, Denmark	L. Heyman	Do.
Yarmouth, Nova Scotia	L. S. Balkam	Do.
Zanzibar, (Island)		Consul.
Do	Francis R. Webb	Vice-consul.
Zacatecas, Mexico	G. M. Prevost	Consul.

LIST OF MINISTERS, CONSULS, ETC.

Consular offices.	Consular officers.	Rank.
Zante, Ionian Isles	A. S. York	Consul.
Zaza, Cuba	D. B. Iznaga	Consular agent.
Zurich, Switzerland	Charles A. Page	Consul.

NOTE.—The consular officers to whom this pamphlet is sent are requested to indicate any inaccuracies which they may notice in the two foregoing lists, and report the same to the Department for correction.

LIST

OF

COMMISSIONS AND CONSULATES GENERAL, CONSULATES GENERAL, CONSULATES, AND COMMERCIAL AGENCIES, WITH THE COMPENSATION ATTACHED TO EACH.

I.—COMMISSIONS AND CONSULATES GENERAL.

Monrovia	$4,000
Port au Prince	7,500

II.—CONSULATES GENERAL.

SCHEDULE B.

Alexandria	3,500
Beirût	2,000
Calcutta	5,000
Constantinople	3,000
Frankfort-on-the-Main	3,000
Havana	6,000
Montreal	4,000
Shanghai	4,000
Tampico	1,500

III.—CONSULATE GENERAL.

SCHEDULE C.

....	....

IV.—CONSULATE GENERAL.

NOT EMBRACED IN SCHEDULE B OR C.

Florence	Fees.

V.—CONSULATES.

SCHEDULE B.

Aix la-Chapelle	2,500
Algiers	$1,500
Amoy	3,000
Amsterdam	1,000
Antwerp	2,500
Aspinwall	2,500
Bangkok	2,000
Barcelona	1,500
Basle	2,000
Belfast	2,000
Brindisi	1,500
Buenos Ayres	2,000
Bordeaux	2,000
Boulogne	1,500
Bremen	3,000
Cadiz	1,500
Callao	3,500
Canea	1,000
Canton	4,000
Chin Kiang	3,000
Chemnitz	2,000
Clifton	1,500
Coaticook	1,500

80 LIST OF MINISTERS, CONSULS, ETC.

Cork	$2,000	Leipsic	$1,50
Demarara	2,000	Lisbon	1,00
Dundee	2,000	Liverpool	7,50
Elsinore	1,500	London	7,50
Foo-Chow	3,500	Lyons	2,00
Fort Erie	1,500	Malaga	1,50
Funchal	1,500	Malta	1,50
Geneva	1,500	Manchester	3,00
Genoa	1,500	Matanzas	2,50
Gibraltar	1,500	Marseilles	2,50
Glasgow	3,000	Mauritius	2,50
Goderich	1,500	Melbourne	4,00
Halifax	2,000	Messina	1,50
Hamburg	2,000	Moscow	2,00
Hankow	3,000	Munich	1,50
Havre	6,000	Nagasaki	3,00
Honolulu	4,000	Nantes	1,50
Hong-Kong	3,500	Naples	1,50
Jerusalem	1,500	Nassau, W. I.	2,00
Kanagawa	3,000	Newcastle	1,50
Kingston, Jamaica	2,000	Nice, France	1,50
Kingston, Canada	1,500	Odessa	2,00
La Rochelle	1,500	Oporto	1,50
Laguayra	1,500	Osacca	3,00
Lahaina	3,000	Palermo	1,50
Leeds	2,000	Panama	3,50
Leghorn	1,500	Paris	5,00

LIST OF MINISTERS, CONSULS, ETC.

81

Pernambuco	$2,000	Swatow	$3,500
Pictou	1,500	Tangier	3,000
Ponce	1,500	Toronto	1,500
Port Mahon	1,500	Trieste	2,000
Port Sarnia	1,500	Trinidad de Cuba	2,500
Prescott	1,500	Tripoli	3,000
Prince Edward Island	1,500	Tunis	3,000
Quebec	1,500	Turk's Islands	2,000
Revel	2,000	Valparaiso	3,000
Rio de Janeiro	6,000	Vera Cruz	3,500
Rome	1,500	Vienna	1,500
Rotterdam	2,000	Windsor, Canada	1,500
San Juan del Sur	2,000	Yeddo	3,000
San Juan, Porto Rico	2,000	Zurich	1,500
Santiago de Cuba	2,500		
Seychelles, Indian Ocean	1,500		

VI.—COMMERCIAL AGENCIES.

SCHEDULE B.

Belize	
Acapulco	2,000
Madagascar, (Tamatave)	2,000
San Juan del Norte	2,000
St. Domingo	1,500
St. Helena	1,500

Singapore	2,500
Smyrna	2,000
Southampton	2,000
St. John's, Canada East	1,500
St. John's, N. F.	
St. Petersburg	2,000
St. Pierre, Martinique	1,500
St. Thomas	4,000
Stuttgard	1,000

VII.—CONSULATES.

SCHEDULE C.*

Aux Cayes	500
Bahia	1,000

*Consular officers residing at all places, except those in schedule B, are permitted to transact business.

11

LIST OF MINISTERS, CONSULS, ETC.

Batavia	$1,000	Santa Cruz	$
Bay of Islands	1,000	Santiago, Cape Verde	750
Cape Haytien	1,000	Spezia	
Cape Town	1,000	Stettin	1,000
Carthagena	500	Tabasco	500
Ceylon	1,000	Tahiti	1,000
Cobija	500	Talcahuano	1,000
Cyprus	1,000	Tumbez	500
Fayal	750	Venice	750
Guayaquil	750	Zanzibar	1,000
Guaymas	1,000		
Lanthala	1,000		
Maranham	1,000		
Matamoras	1,000		
Mexico	1,000		
Montevideo	1,000		
Omoa	1,000		
Payta	500		
Para	1,000		
Paso del Norte	500		
Piræus	1,000		
Port Stanley, Falkland Islands	1,000		
Rio Grande	1,000		
Sabanilla	500		
St. Catharine	1,000		

VIII.—COMMERCIAL AGENCIES.

SCHEDULE C.

Amoor River	1,000
Apia	1,000
Gaboon	1,000
St. Paul de Loando	1,000

IX.—CONSULATES NOT EMBRACED IN SCHEDULE B OR C.*

Alicante	Fees.
Altona	Fees.
Aguas Calientes	Fees.
Ancona	Fees.
Archangel	Fees.
Arica	Fees.
Asuncion	Fees.

* Consular officers residing at all places, except those in schedule B, are permitted to transact business.

LIST OF MINISTERS, CONSULS, ETC.

83

Athens	Fees.	Curaçoa	Fees.
Augsburg	Fees.	Denia	Fees.
Barbadoes	Fees.	Dresden	Fees.
Bathhurst	Fees.	Dublin	Fees.
Bergen	Fees.	Falmouth	Fees.
Bermuda	Fees.	Galatza	Fees.
Bilbao	Fees.	Galway	Fees.
Biscao	Fees.	Gaspé Basin	Fees.
Bogota	Fees.	Geestemunde	Fees.
Bombay	Fees.	Ghent	Fees.
Bristol	Fees.	Gottenburg	Fees.
Brunai	Fees.	Guadaloupe	Fees.
Brunswick	Fees.	Guatemala	Fees.
Brussels	Fees.	Hamilton	Fees.
Bucharest	Fees.	Helsingfors	Fees.
Cairo	Fees.	Hesse Cassel	Fees.
Campeachy	Fees.	Hesse Darmstadt	Fees.
Cardiff	Fees.	Hesse Hombourg	Fees.
Carlsruhe	Fees.	Hobart Town	Fees.
Carrara	Fees.	Hilo	Fees.
Carthagena, Spain	Fees.	Kiu Kiang	Fees.
Cayenne	Fees.	Lambayeque	Fees.
Chee-Foo	Fees.	Laguna	Fees.
Cihuahua	Fees.	La Paz	Fees.
Ciudad Bolivar	Fees.	La Union	Fees.
Copenhagen	Fees.	Leith	Fees.
Coquimbo	Fees.	Liege	Fees.

84   LIST OF MINISTERS, CONSULS, ETC.

Londonderry	Fees.	Rhenish Bavaria	Fees.
Lubec	Fees.	Riga	Fees.
Macao	Fees.	Rio Hacha	Fees.
Manila	Fees.	Rio Negro	Fees.
Manzanillo	Fees.	San Luis Potosi	Fees.
Maracaibo	Fees.	Saltillo	Fees.
Mazatlan	Fees.	San Blas	Fees.
Merida and Sisal	Fees.	San José	Fees.
Monterey	Fees.	Santa Martha	Fees.
Mozambique	Fees.	Santander	Fees.
Muscat	Fees.	Santos	Fees.
Napoléon Vendée	Fees.	Schwerin	Fees
Nassau, Europe	Fees.	Scio	Fees
New Chwang	Fees.	Seville	Fees
Ningpo	Fees.	Sheffield	Fees
Nuremburg	Fees.	Sonneberg	Fees
Oldenburg	Fees.	St. John, N. B.	Fees
Ostend	Fees.	St. Martin	Fees
Otranto	Fees.	Strasbourg	Fees
Padang	Fees.	St. Thomé, Africa	Fees
Parnahiba	Fees.	Stockholm	Fees
Paramaribo	Fees.	Sydney, N. S. W.	Fee
Plymouth	Fees.	Taranto	Fee
Porsgrund	Fees.	Tehuantepec	Fee
Puerto Cabello	Fees.	Teneriffe	Fee
Ravenna	Fees.	Tien-Tsin	Fee
Reims	Fees.	Trebisond	Fee

LIST OF MINISTERS, CONSULS, ETC.

85

Trinidad	Fees.	Comayagua and Tegucigalpa	Fees.
Turbo	Fees.	Grand Bassa	Fees.
Valencia	Fees.	Hakodadi	Fees.
Verviers	Fees.	Medellin	Fees.
Victoria, V. I	Fees.	Minatitlan	Fees.
Vigo	Fees.	Punta Arenas	Fees.
Zacatecas	Fees.	Rosario	Fees.
Zante	Fees.	Roseau, Dominica	Fees.
		St. Bartholomew	Fees.

X.—COMMERCIAL AGENCIES NOT EMBRACED IN SCHEDULE B OR C.

		St. Christopher	Fees.
Antigua	Fees.	St. Marc	Fees.
Bradford	Fees.	St. Pierre, Miquelon	Fees.
Carlisle	Fees.	Tetuan	Fees.

LIST

OF

THE DIPLOMATIC OFFICERS OF THE UNITED STATES IN FOREIGN COUNTRIES, WITH THE COMPENSATION ATTACHED TO THEM, RESPECTIVELY.

(Corrected to August, 1868.)

Countries.	Rank.	Compensation.
Argentine Republic	Minister Resident	$7,500
	Secretary of Legation	1,500
Austria	Envoy Extraordinary and Minister Plenipotentiary	12,000
	Secretary of Legation	1,800
Belgium	Minister Resident	7,500
	Secretary of Legation	1,500
Bolivia	Minister Resident	7,500
	Secretary of Legation	1,500
Brazil	Envoy Extraordinary and Minister Plenipotentiary	12,000
	Secretary of Legation	1,800
Chili	Envoy Extraordinary and Minister Plenipotentiary	10,000
	Secretary of Legation	1,500
China	Envoy Extraordinary and Minister Plenipotentiary	12,000
	Secretary of Legation { acting as Interpreter	5,000
	not acting as Interpreter	3,000
Costa Rica	Minister Resident	7,500
	Secretary of Legation	1,500
Denmark	Minister Resident	7,500
	Secretary of Legation	1,500

LIST OF MINISTERS, CONSULS, ETC.

Countries.	Rank.	Compensation
Ecuador	Minister Resident	$7,5
	Secretary of Legation	1,5
France	Envoy Extraordinary and Minister Plenipotentiary	17,5
	Secretary of Legation	2,6
	Assistant Secretary of Legation	1,5
Great Britain	Envoy Extraordinary and Minister Plenipotentiary	17,5
	Secretary of Legation	2,6
	Assistant Secretary of Legation	1,5
Guatemala	Minister Resident	7,5
	Secretary of Legation	1,5
Hawaiian Islands	Minister Resident	7,5
Hayti	Minister Resident and Consul General	7,5
Honduras	Minister Resident	7,5
Italy	Envoy Extraordinary and Minister Plenipotentiary	12,0
	Secretary of Legation	1,8
Japan	Minister Resident	7,5
	Secretary of Legation, acting as Interpreter	2,5
Liberia	Minister Resident and Consul General	4,0
Mexico	Envoy Extraordinary and Minister Plenipotentiary	12,0
	Secretary of Legation	1,8
Netherlands	Minister Resident	7,5
	Secretary of Legation	1,5
Nicaragua	Minister Resident	7,5
	Secretary of Legation	1,5
Paraguay	Minister Resident	7,5

LIST OF MINISTERS, CONSULS, ETC.

89

Countries.	Rank.		Compensation.
Peru	Envoy Extraordinary and Minister Plenipotentiary..		$10,000
	Secretary of Legation		1,500
Portugal	Minister Resident		
	Secretary of Legation		1,500
Prussia	Envoy Extraordinary and Minister Plenipotentiary..		12,000
	Secretary of Legation		1,800
Russia	Envoy Extraordinary and Minister Plenipotentiary..		12,000
	Secretary of Legation		1,800
Salvador	Minister Resident		7,500
	Secretary of Legation		1,500
Spain	Envoy Extraordinary and Minister Plenipotentiary..		12,000
	Secretary of Legation		1,800
Sweden and Norway	Minister Resident		7,500
	Secrétary of Legation		1,500
Switzerland	Minister Resident		7,500
	Secretary of Legation		1,500
Turkey	Minister Resident		7,500
	Secretary of Legation. {	acting as Dragoman	3,000
		not acting as Dragoman....	2,000
	Dragoman, when Secretary of Legation is not acting as such		1,000
United States of Colombia..	Minister Resident		7,500
	Secretary of Legation		1,500
Venezuela	Minister Resident		7,500
	Secretary of Legation		1,500

12

SUMMARY.

DIPLOMATIC OFFICERS.

Envoys Extraordinary and Ministers Plenipotentiary	13
Ministers Resident	20
Ministers Resident and Consul General	2
Secretaries of Legation	13
Assistant Secretaries of Legation	2
Secretary of Legation and Dragoman	1
Interpreters	2
Secretary of Legation and Interpreter	1
	—— 54

CONSULAR OFFICERS.

Consuls General	9
Vice-Consuls General	7
Consuls	243
Deputy Consuls	11
Commercial Agents	41
Vice-Consuls	000
Consular Agents	297
Vice-Commercial Agents	10
Agents of Commercial Agents	3
Interpreters	3
Marshals of Consular Courts	5
Deputy Marshal of Consular Court	1
Consular Clerks	13
	—— 643

JUDICIAL OFFICERS.

Judges	3
Arbitrators	3
	—— 6
Aggregate	703

DIPLOMATIC CORPS.

LIST OF FOREIGN MINISTERS ACCREDITED TO THE GOVERNMENT OF THE UNITED STATES, AND OF THEIR SECRETARIES AND ATTACHÉS.

GREAT BRITAIN.

Edward Thornton, esquire, envoy extraordinary and minister plenipotentiary, corner I and Conn. avenue.
—— ——, esquire, secretary of legation, 30 L street, (absent.)
——, second secretary, —— streets.
Mr. Peere Williams Freeman, second secretary, 252 I street.
Mr. W. Fane, second secretary, the British legation.
Henry Howard, esquire, attaché, I street near 17th street.

FRANCE.

M. J. Berthemy, envoy extraordinary and minister plenipotentiary, corner of H and 15th streets, Washington, D. C.
Comte de Turrene, second secretary.
Vicomte d'Aulers, attaché, 493 17th street.
Chevalier Roger de La Laude, corner 19th and Penn. avenue, attaché.
M. P. Dejardin, chancellier, corner 14th and I streets.

RUSSIA.

Mr. Edward de Stoeckl, envoy extraordinary and minister plenipotentiary, 173 Penn. avenue.
Mr. Waldemar de Bodisco, first secretary, chargé d'affaires, 149 West street, Georgetown, D. C.
Mr. Boris Danzas, second secretary, (absent on leave.)
Mr. Constantin de Bodisco, attaché, Road street, between Washington and Congress streets, Georgetown, D. C.

NETHERLANDS.

M. A. Mazel, minister resident, 248½ G street, near 17th street.

SPAIN.

Señor Don Facundo Goñi, envoy extraordinary and minister plenipotentiary, 363 corner 14th and H streets, Washington, D. C.
Señor Don Luis de Potestad, first secretary, 137 West st., Georgetown.
Señor Don Enrique Vallés, second secretary.
Señor Don P. Diez de Rivera, attaché, No. 456 New York avenue, Washington, D. C.

DIPLOMATIC CORPS.

AUSTRIA.

Le Baron de Franckenstein, chargé d'affaires *ad interim*, 159 Penn: avenue, Washington, D. C.

PRUSSIA.

Baron von Gerolt, envoy extraordinary and minister plenipotentiary No. 423 15th street, Washington, D. C.

Count Lottom, No. 185 G street near 19th street, Washington, D. C

P. W. Büddocke, acting chancellor, 319 D street, between 11th an 12th streets, Washington, D. C.

ITALY.

The Chevalier Marcello Cerruti, envoy extraordinary and ministe plenipotentiary, 159 Pensylvania avenue.

Mr. R. Cantagalli, secretary of legation, (absent.)

SWEDEN AND NORWAY.

Baron de Wetterstedt, envoy extraordinary and minister plenipotentiary

DENMARK.

F. E. Bille, chargé d'affaires, 178 G street, between 19th and 20th streets Washington.

PORTUGAL.

Mr. Miguel Martins d'Antas, envoy extraordinary and minister pleni potentiary, (absent.)

Mr. Manoel Garcia da Roza, chargé d'affaires *ad interim*, 431 corne of I and 14th streets, Washington, D. C.

BELGIUM.

Mr. Maurice Delfosse, minister resident, No. 157 Pennsylvania avenue Washington, D. C.

GUATEMALA AND SALVADOR.

NICARAGUA AND HONDURAS.

Don Ignacio Gomez, minister resident and E. E., 402 16th street Washington.

DIPLOMATIC CORPS.

COSTA RICA.

Don Ezequiel Gutierrez, chargé d'affaires, 422 15th street, Washington, D. C.

BRAZIL.

The Councillor Domingos José Gonsalves de Magalhaens, E. E. and M. P., 15th street near I street.
Senhor Luiz Auguste de Padua Fleury, attaché of the 1st class.
Don Benjamin Franklin Torreao de Barros, attaché of the 1st class.

MEXICO.

———, envoy extraordinary and minister plenipotentiary.
———, secretary of legation, chargé d'affaires.
Señor Cayetano Romero, attaché.

CHILI.

Señor Mariano Sanchez Fontecilla, chargé d'affaires, Washington.
Señor Juan Eduardo Mackenna, secretary of legation.
Señor Carlos Walker Martinez, attaché.

VENEZUELA.

Señor Blas Bruzual, envoy extraordinary and minister plenipotentiary, (absent,) 35 west 33d street, New York.
Señor Florencio Ribas, secretary of legation and chargé d'affaires *ad interim*, 5½ Pine street, New York.
Commander José J. Roldan, first attaché.
Señor Abraham J. Dorale, second attaché.

UNITED STATES OF COLOMBIA.

——— ———, E. E. and M. P., (absent.)

PERU.

Señor Don José Antonio Garcia y Garcia, envoy extraordinary and minister plenipotentiary, Clarendon Hotel, New York.
Mr. A. Benjamin Medina, first secretary of legation.
Mr. George B. Robinson, attaché.

LIBERIA.

Henry M. Schieffelin, esquire, chargé d'affaires, 22 Bible House, New York.
William Coppinger, secretary of legation.

94 DIPLOMATIC CORPS.

HAWAIIAN ISLANDS.

Charles C. Harris, esquire, E. E. and M. P.

HAYTI.

George Raester, chargé d'affaires and consul general, 132 Front street New York.

George Lawrence, jr., in the employ of the legation.

ARGENTINE.

Don Bartolome Mitre y Vedia, secretary of legation, chargé d'affaire *ad interim.*

Don Alberto A. Halbach, attaché of the 1st class.

Don Domingo E. de Sarratea, attaché.

GREECE.

Mr. Alexandre Rizo Rangabé, E. E., (absent.)

Mr. Cleon Rizo Rangabé, secretary, 252 G street, Washington.

TURKEY.

Blacque Bey, E. E. & M. P., 361 H street, Washington, D. C.

Mr. Xenophon Baltazzi, secretary, 298 F street, between 12th and 13tl streets, Washington, D. C.

LIST

OF

FOREIGN CONSULS IN THE UNITED STATES.

Name.	Title.	Residence.
GREAT BRITAIN.		
Arthur T. Lynn	Consul	Galveston.
George Moore	Do	Richmond.
H. T. A. Rainals	Do	Baltimore.
F. J. Cridland	· Do	Mobile.
Henry P. Walker	Do	Charleston.
Wm. T. Smith	Do	Savannah.
H. W. Hemans	Do	Buffalo.
Dennis Donohoe	Do	New Orleans.
Francis Lousada	Do	Boston.
John E. Wilkins	Do	Chicago.
E. M. Archibald	Do	New York City.
Henry J. Murray	Do	Portland.
Charles E. K. Kortright	Do	Philadelphia.
Wm. L. Booker	Do	San Francisco.
FRANCE.		
L. de la Forest	Consul	Mobile.
P. Schisano	Vice-consul	Norfolk..
I. Lombard	Consular agent	Monterey.
F. Gourand	Vice-consul	Newport and Providence, R. I.
L. P. Le Prohon	Consular agent	Portland.

LIST OF FOREIGN CONSULAR OFFICERS, ETC.

Name.	Title.	Residence.
Gauldreé Boilleau	Consul general	New York.
Chas. F. de Cazotte	Consul	San Francisco.
E. N. M. Godeaux	Do	New Orleans.
H. P. de St. Cyr	Vice-consular agent	Galveston.
Jules Phillippe	Vice-consular agent	Mobile.
Ravin d'Elpeux	Vice-consular agent	Cincinnati.
Edmund Carrey	Vice-consul	Chicago.
J. N. Perrier	Consular agent	Newport, R. I.
Chas. Fauconnet	Vice-consul	Galveston.
J. E. Sanchard	Consul	Boston.
F. C. A. L. de LaForrest	Do	Philadelphia.
J. J. Perrin	Consular agent	Louisville.
Leon Schisano	Do	Norfolk.
H. Levasseur	Vice-consular agent	St. Louis.
Armand Peugnet	Vice-consul	Cincinnati.
Amedée Sauvan	Do	Baltimore.
Fernando Moreno	Do	Key West.
J. A. H. Poitevin	Consular agent	Mobile.
Frederic Chastanet	Do	Savannah.
Jacob Loeb	Do	Wilmington, N. C.
Alexander B. de Bughas	Consul	Charleston, S. C.
Jean Baptiste Sauvan	Do	Richmond.
RUSSIA.		
Edward Johns	Consul	New Orleans.
J. R. Wilder	Vice-consul	Savannah.

LIST OF FOREIGN CONSULAR OFFICERS ETC.

97

Name.	Title.	Residence.
R. B. Storer	Vice-consul	Boston.
J. Leland	Do	Charleston.
Augustus Kohler	Do	Baltimore.
Ferdinand Wolff	Do	Galveston.
M. Klinkowstrœm	Do	San Francisco.
Chas. von der Osten Sacken	Consul general	New York.
Robert Schultze	Vice-consul	New York.
Henry Préaut	Do	Philadelphia.
Johann F. Schroder	Do	New Orleans.
A. I. Kleinbach	Do	Mobile.
Post Capt'n Prince Maksioutoff	Consul	Sitkha.
PRUSSIA.		
Geo. Hussey	Vice-consul	New Bedford.
F. A. Hirsch	Do	Boston.
J. W. Jockusch	Consul	Galveston.
J. Von Borries	Do	Louisville.
H. Claussenius	Do	Chicago.
Adolph Rosenthal	Do	Milwaukee.
Werner Dressel	Do	Baltimore.
I. H. Gossler, jr	Do	Boston.
C. F. Adae	Do	Cincinnati.
E. von der Heydt	Do	New York.
H. Hanssmann	Do	San Francisco.
Robert Barth	Do	St. Louis.
Jean Kruttschnitt	Do	New Orleans.

13

98 LIST OF FOREIGN CONSULAR OFFICERS, ETC.

Name.	Title.	Residence.
F. Schuster	Consul	Savannah.
F. W. Hanewinckel	Do	Richmond.
Robert W. Welch	Vice-consul	Key West.
Guido von Grabow	Consul General	New York.
Carl Vezin	Consul	Philadelphia.
W. H. Trappmann	Do	Charleston.
Ferdinand Willius	Do	St. Paul, Minn.
AUSTRIA.		
Adolfus Bader	Consul	New Orleans.
J. E. Dumont	Vice-consul	Mobile.
A. Low	Do	Savannah.
S. M. Waln	Do	Philadelphia.
Charles Loosey	Consul	New York.
Moritz Baumbach	Vice-consul	Milwaukee.
Julius Kaufman	Do	Galveston.
Robert Barth	Do	St. Louis.
Edward W. de Voss	Do	Richmond.
Charles F. Loosey	Consul general	New York.
Edward T. Hardy	Vice-consul	Norfolk.
F. D. Kremelberg	Do	Baltimore.
I. H. Gossler	Do	Boston.
ITALY.		
Ferdinando de Luca	Consul general	New York.
Gustavo M. Finotti	Consular agent	Boston.
G. B. Cerruti	Consul	San Francisco.

LIST OF FOREIGN CONSULAR OFFICERS, ETC.

99

Name.	Title.	Residence.
Duncan Robertson	Consul	Norfolk.
Alonzo Viti	Vice-consul	Philadelphia.
F. Sanminiatelli	Do	New Orleans.
G. L. Avezzana	Do	New York.
Nicholas Reggio	Do	Boston.
L. A. J. B. Paris	Do	St. Louis.
C. A. Williamson	Do	Baltimore.
Nicola Nicholas	Do	Louisville.
G. A. Signaigo	Do	Memphis.
Daniel von Groning	Do	Richmond.
Giorgio Aite	Do	Mobile.
Carlo F. Jenni	Do	Galveston.
Natale Piazza	Do	Vicksburg.
E. L. Trenholm	Do	Charleston.
William Pinkney	Do	Key West.
David Tandy	Consular agent	St. Louis.
Augusto Fredin	Do	Chicago.
Giovanni L. Cella	Do	Do.
SPAIN.		
Don Pablo Chacon	Consul general	Philadelphia.
J. A. Pizarro	Vice-consul	Baltimore.
A. G. Vega	Consul	Boston.
D. Robertson	Vice-consul	Norfolk.
Robert H. Betts	Do	St. Louis.
Benj. Theron	Do	Galveston.

100 LIST OF FOREIGN CONSULAR OFFICERS, ETC.

Name.	Title.	Residence.
A. Vinyals	Consul	Charleston.
Robert O. Treadwell	Vice-consul	Portsmouth, N. H.
Don J. de A. Sanmartin	Do	New Orleans.
Camilo Martin	Do	San Francisco.
Vincente Cubells	Consul	Key West.
Luis Casaval	Vice-consul	Savannah.
Frederico Granados	Vice-consul	Boston.
F. de Carpiy Cabrera	Do	New York.
Isidoro Millas	Consul	New Orleans.
Antonio M. de Zea	Do.	Portland, Me.
C. L. le Barron	Vice-consul	Pensacola.
Ramon Orbeta.	Consul.	Mobile.
Agustin Rodriguez	Do.	Galveston.
José A. de Lavalle	Do.	Philadelphia.
J. M. de Satrustegui	Do.	New York.
Ignatius Sargent	Vice-consul	Machias, Me.
Ebenezer T. Fox	Consul	Bangor, Me.

TURKEY.

J. Jasigi	Consul	Boston.
George A. Porter	Do.	Washington and Baltimore.
C. Oscanyan	Consul general	New York.
J. Hosford Smith	Consul.	New York.

SWEDEN AND NORWAY.

D. Robertson	Vice-consul	Virginia.
James Dempsey	Do.	Alexandria.

LIST OF FOREIGN CONSULAR OFFICERS, ETC. 101

Name.	Title.	Residence.
R. Westfeldt	Vice-consul	Mobile.
P. L. Hawkinson	Do.	Chicago.
E. S. Sayres	Do.	Philadelphia.
John E. Schuetze	Do.	St. Louis.
C. E. Habicht	Consul	New York.
Theodore Borup	Vice-consul	St. Paul, Minn.
C. O. Nilsen	Do.	La Crosse, Wis.
C. O. Witte	Do.	Charleston.
S. M. Svenson	Do.	New Orleans.
C. M. Holst	Do.	Savannah.
K. Y. Fleischer	Do.	Madison, Wis.
Gjert Lootz	Do.	Boston.
J. F. Packer	Do.	Key West.
C. C. Johnson	Consul general.	San Francisco.
S. Palm	Vice-consul	Austin, Texas.
C. Schwarzkopf	Do.	Norfolk.
William M. Perkins	Do.	New Orleans.
Martin Lewis	Do.	Baltimore.
G. T. Lommen.	Do.	Decorah, Iowa.
G. O'Hara Taaffe	Do.	San Francisco.
Geo. H. Garlichs	Do.	Cincinnati.
Chas. G. Youngberg	Do.	New York.
C. F. Boysen	Do.	Pensacola.

NETHERLANDS.

J. Myers	Consul	Norfolk.

102 LIST OF FOREIGN CONSULAR OFFICERS, ETC.

Name.	Title.	Residence.
O. O. Hara	Vice-consul	Key West.
J. I. Van Wanroy	Consul	Mobile.
Amedée Conturié	Do.	New Orleans.
Rudolph C. Burlage	Consul general	New York.
Claas Vocke	Consul	Baltimore.
Nicholaus Anslyn	Vice-consul	Keokuk, Iowa.
J. F. V. Dorselin	Consul	Wis., Mich., Minn.
Carl Epping	Vice-consul	Savannah.
J. E. Zimmerman	Vice-consul general	New York.
J. de Fremery	Consul	San Francisco.
G. H. Garlichs	Do.	Cincinnati.
B. B. Haagsma	Do.	St. Louis.
Alfred Schucking	Vice-consul	Washington, D. C.
G. Lootz	Consul	At Boston, for Mass., Maine, N. Hamp., and R. Island.
Chas. E. Wunderlich	Do.	Charleston.
L. Westergaard	Do.	Philadelphia.
BELGIUM.		
H. W. T. Mali	Consul general	New York.
T. A. Deblois	Consul	Portland.
W. G. Porter	Vice-consul	Apalachicola.
W. O'Driscoll	Consul	Savannah.
G. O. Gorter	Do.	Baltimore.
Emlie Grisar	Do.	San Francisco.
P. Schuster	Do.	Cincinnati.
J. G. Bates	Do	Boston.

LIST OF FOREIGN CONSULAR OFFICERS, ETC.

103

Name.	Title.	Residence.
Gustave E. Matile	Vice-consul	Philadelphia.
H. W. Mali	Consul	New York.
A. Heydecker	Do	Galveston.
P. Hurck	Do	St. Louis.
Moris Seligman	Do	Charleston.
Emile O. Nolting	Do	Richmond.
J. F. Henrotin	Do	Chicago.
John B. A. Massé	Do	Green Bay, Wisconsin.
H. V. H. Voorhees	Do	Mobile.
Ch. T. van der Espt	Vice-consul	Louisville.
Duncan Robertson	Consul	Norfolk.
Auguste Noblom	Vice-consul	New Orleans.
Laurent De Give	Consul	Atlanta, Ga.
G. E. Saurmann	Do	Philadelphia.
Charles Mali	Do	New York.
J. A. Quintero	Do	New Orleans.
PORTUGAL.		
William H. Allen	Vice-consul	St. Augustine.
Jule Pescay	Do	Pensacola.
Wm. Lord de Rosset	Do	Wilmington.
C. Le Baron	Do	Mobile.
John Searle	Consul	San Francisco.
E. S. Sayres	Vice-consul	Philadelphia.
Robert Lehr	Do	Baltimore.
José M. Bernes	Do	Springfield, Ill.

104 LIST OF FOREIGN CONSULAR OFFICERS, ETC.

Name.	Title.	Residence.
Thos. J. Stewart	Vice-consul	Bangor, Me.
George Hussey, jr	Do.	New Bedford, Mass.
A. M. da C. S. Maior	Consul general	
Archibald Foster	Vice-consul	Boston.
Antonio J. da Silva	Do.	New Orleans.
Ludwig E. Amsinck	Do.	New York.
Joaquin de Palma	Do.	Savannah.
Nathaniel Burruss	Do.	Norfolk.
Wm. W. Harris	Do.	New London, Conn.
Pierre J. Esnard	Do.	Charleston.
DENMARK.		
James Dempsey	Vice-consul	Alexandria.
H. Frellsen	Consul	New Orleans.
J. F. Meline	Vice-consul	Cincinnati.
John E. Schuetz	Do.	St. Louis.
E. S. Sayres	Do.	Philadelphia.
J. C. Kondrup	Do.	Washington, D. C.
E. C. Hammer	Do.	Boston.
C. F. J. Möller	Do.	Milwaukee.
John E. Brown	Do.	Bath, Me.
Henry Braëm	Do.	New York City.
Harold Dollner	Consul	New York City.
Emil Dreier	Vice-consul	Chicago.
Theodore Borup	Do.	St. Paul.
G. O'Hara Taaffe	Consul	San Francisco.

LIST OF FOREIGN CONSULAR OFFICERS, ETC.

Name.	Title.	Residence.
C. M. Holst	Vice-consul	Savannah.
Chas. E. Wunderlich	Do.	Charleston.
S. H. Holmes	Do.	Pensacola.
Martin Lewis	Do.	Baltimore.
Silas N. Martin	Do.	Wilmington, N. C.
Robert B. Searing	Do.	Mobile.
George H. Garlichs	Do.	Cincinnati.
Geo. C. Reid	Do.	Norfolk, Va.
BAVARIA.		
G. H. Siemon	Consul	New York.
C. F. Hagedorn	Consul general	Philadelphia.
J. Smidt	Consul	Louisville.
C. F. Adae	Do.	Cincinnati.
C. F. Mebius	Do.	San Francisco.
Werner Dressel	Do.	Baltimore.
L. von Baumbach	Do.	Milwaukee.
Adolph Bader	Consul	New Orleans.
Robert Barth	Do.	St. Louis.
M. von Baumbach	Vice-consul	Milwaukee.
John Schumacher	Consul	Boston.
SWITZERLAND.		
L. P. de Luze	Consul	New York.
John Hitz	Consul general	Washington.
Adrien Iselin	Vice-consul	New York.
A. Piaget	Consul	New Orleans.

106 LIST OF FOREIGN CONSULAR OFFICERS, ETC.

Name.	Title.	Residence.
Henri Rosenberg	Vice-consul	Galveston.
R. Korradi	Consul	Philadelphia.
P. J. Wildberger	Vice-consul	Do.
Constant Rilliet	Consul	Highland, Illinois.
C. F. Mathey	Do	St. Louis.
David C. Jaccard	Vice-consul	Do.
Henri Enderis	Consul	Chicago.
Henri Meyer	Do	Charleston.
Alexis de Stouts	Vice-consul	San Francisco.
Louis Boerlin	Do	Chicago.
Jacques Rietschy	Consul	Cincinnati.
François Berton	Do	San Francisco.
Antoine Borel	Vice consul	Do.
SAXONY.		
Charles J. Cazenove	Vice-consul	Boston.
C. F. Adae	Consul	Cincinnati.
Werner Dresel	Do	Baltimore.
Robert Barth	Do	St. Louis.
Johann W. Schmidt	Consul general	New York.
Theodor Schwartz	Consul	Louisville, Ky.
Herman Michels	Do	San Francisco.
H. Claussenius	Do	Chicago.
Chas. H. Pandorf	Do	New Orleans.
Leopold Schmidt	Do	New York.
M. von Baumbach	Do	Milwaukee.

LIST OF FOREIGN CONSULAR OFFICERS, ETC.

Name.	Title.	Residence.
H. T. Plate	Consul	Philadelphia.
Julius Kauffmann	Do	Galveston.
GREECE.		
J. M. Rodocanachi	Consul	Boston.
D. N. Botassis	Do	New York.
Nicholas Benachi	Do	New Orleans.
C. P. Ralli	Vice-consul	St. Louis.
PONTIFICAL STATES.		
W. D. Senac	Vice-consul	Norfolk.
H. Perrot	Do	New Orleans.
S. Wright	Do	Savannah.
J. P. Scott	Do	Baltimore.
N. Reggio	Do	Boston.
Alexis Robert	Consul	New Orleans.
L. B. Binsse	Consul general	New York.
J. F. Meline	Vice-consul	Cincinnati.
Geo. Allen	Do	Philadelphia.
Edward Mottet	Do	Charleston.
WURTEMBURG.		
F. A. Sauters	Consul	Galveston.
Robert Barth	Do	St. Louis, Mo.
Isaac Wormser	Do	San Francisco.
A. Widenmann	Do	Ann Harbor, Michigan.
Friederich Klumpp	Do	New Orleans.
Leopold Bierwirth	Consul general	New York.

108 LIST OF FOREIGN CONSULAR OFFICERS, ETC.

Name.	Title.	Residence.
Carl F. Adae	Consul	Cincinnati.
John Smidt	Do	Louisville, Ky.
L. von Baumbach	Do	Milwaukee, Wis.
Werner Dresel	Do	Baltimore.
Wm. L. Kiderlen	Do	Philadelphia.

BADEN.

Name.	Title.	Residence.
Leopold Schmidt	Consul general	For the United States.
L. von Baumbach	Consul	Milwaukee.
Werner Dresel	Consul	Baltimore.
Leopold Schmidt	Vice-consul	New York.
John Smidt	Consul	Louisville, Ky.
C. F. Adae	Do	Cincinnati.
Adolf Bader	Do	New Orleans.
Robert Barth	Do	St. Louis.
H. Hanssmann	Do	San Francisco.
M. von Baumbach	Vice-consul	Milwaukee.
C. F. Hagedorn	Consul	Philadelphia.

HESSE DARMSTADT.

Name.	Title.	Residence.
F. W. Keutgen	Consul	New York.
L. von Baumbach	Do	Milwaukee.
Robert Barth	Do	St. Louis, Mo.
John Smidt	Do	Louisville.
C. F. Adae	Do	Cincinnati.
Gustav Ziel	Do	San Francisco.
Heinrich Möser	Do	Pittsburg.

LIST OF FOREIGN CONSULAR OFFICERS, ETC. 109

Name.	Title.	Residence.
M. von Baumbach	Vice-consul	Milwaukee.
August Beck	Consul	Chicago.
C. F. Hagedorn	Consul general	Philadelphia.
August Reichard	Consul	New Orleans.
J. W. Iockush	Vice-consul	Galveston.
Werner Dresel	Consul	Baltimore.
MECKLENBURG SCHWERIN.		
August Reichard	Consul	New Orleans.
H. Schultz	Consul and commercial agent.	Galveston.
J. de Fremery	Consul	San Francisco.
George Papendiek	Do	Boston.
F. H. Harjes	Do	Philadelphia.
C. F. Adae	Do	Cincinnati.
H. Claussenius	Do	Chicago.
Robert Barth	Do	St. Louis.
M. von Baumbach	Vice-consul	Milwaukee.
L. von Baumbach	Consul	Do.
Friedrich Kuhne	Consul general	New York.
MECKLENBURG STRELITZ.		
Friedrich Kuhne	Consul	New York.
Carl F. Adae	Do	Cincinnati.
OLDENBURG.		
J. Frederich	Consul	Galveston.
C. F. Adae	Do	Cincinnati.
J. W. Schmidt	Consul general	New York.

110 LIST OF FOREIGN CONSULAR OFFICERS, ETC.

Name.	Title.	Residence.
Theodore Schwartz	Consul	Louisville.
C. E. Wunderlich	Do.	Charleston.
Robert Barth	Do.	St. Louis.
R. W. Welch	Vice-consul	Key West.
C. F. Hagedorn	Consul	Philadelphia.
H. O. S. Cuntz	Do.	Boston.
L. von Baumbach	Do.	Milwaukee.
Charles Bulling	Do.	Baltimore.
Heinrich Muller	Do.	Savannah.
H. Hanssmann	Do.	San Francisco.
Ferdinand Motz	Do.	New Orleans.
M. von Baumbach	Vice-consul	Milwaukee.
BRUNSWICK AND LUNEBURG.		
G. J. Bechtel	Consul general	New York.
Adolph Rosenthal	Consul	Milwaukee.
Robert Barth	Do.	St Louis.
Herman Beckurts	Do.	
F. A. Hoffman	Do.	Chicago.
Adolph Rettberg	Do.	Cleveland, Ohio.
Carl Schmidt	Do.	Cincinnati.
Joseph Lang	Do.	New Orleans.
C. F. Hagedorn	Do.	Philadelphia.
SAXE WEIMAR.		
Julius Sampson	Consul	Mobile.
F. A. Hoffman	Do.	Chicago.

LIST OF FOREIGN CONSULAR OFFICERS, ETC.

Name.	Title.	Residence.
C. F. Hagedorn	Consul	District of Columbia.
M. von Baumbach	Do	Milwaukee.
G. H. Garlichs	Do	Cincinnati.
Robert Barth	Do	St. Louis, Mo.
Frederick Kuhne	Consul general	New York.
Hermann Michals	Consul	San Francisco.
SAXE ALTENBURG.		
Carl E. L. Hinrichs	Consul	New York.
Friederich Kuhne	Vice-consul	New York.
C. F. Adae	Consul	Cincinnati.
Robert Barth	Do	St. Louis.
H. Claussenius	Do	Chicago.
M. von Baumbach	Do	Milwaukee.
SAXE MEININGEN.		
Friederich Kuhne	Consul	New York.
C. F. Adae	Do	Cincinnati.
M. von Baumbach	Do	Milwaukee.
F. A. Hoffmann	Do	Chicago.
Hermann Michels	Do	San Francisco.
SAXE COBURG AND GOTHA.		
C. E. L. Hinrichs	Consul	New York.
Charles Schmidt	Do	Cincinnati.
Adalbert Moeller	Do	La Crosse, Wisconsin.
Friederich Kuhne	Do	New York.
F. A. Hoffmann	Do	Chicago.

112   LIST OF FOREIGN CONSULAR OFFICERS, ETC.

Name.	Title.	Residence.
Robert Barth	Consul	St. Louis.
Herman Michels	Do	San Francisco.
C. F. Hagedorn	Do	Philadelphia.
SCHWARZBURG SONDERS-HAUSEN.		
Friedrich Kuhne	Consul	New York.
Adolph Rosenthal	Do	Milwaukee.
H. Claussenius	Do	Chicago.
SCHWARZBURG RUDOL-STADT.		
Friedrich Kuhne	Consul	New York.
Adolph Rosenthal	Do	Milwaukee.
H. Claussenius	Do	Chicago.
REUSS, ELDER LINE.		
Friedrich Kuhne	Consul	New York.
REUSS, YOUNGER LINE.		
Friedrich Kuhne	Consul	New York.
Adolf Rosenthal	Do	Milwaukee.
Guido Fuchs	Do	Baltimore.
SCHAUMBERG LIPPE.		
Carl Messing	Consul	Philadelphia.
Godfrey Snydacker	Do	Chicago.
C. F. Adae	Do	Cincinnati.
LIPPE, PRINCIPALITY OF.		
Friedrich Kuhne	Consul	New York.
ANHALT-DESSAU.		
Friedrich Kuhne	Consul	New York.

LIST OF FOREIGN CONSULAR OFFICERS, ETC.

Name.	Title.	Residence.
H. Claussenius	Consul	Chicago.
Adolph Rosenthal.................	Do...............	Milwaukee.
HAMBURG.		
C. Knorre......................	Vice-consul	Boston.
F. Rodewald	Consul	Baltimore.
A. Schumacher	Consul general	Baltimore.
H. Ludlam.....................	Consul	Richmond.
J. W. Jockusch..................	Do...............	Galveston.
H. Runge	Do...............	Indianola, Texas.
H. A. Schroeder	Do...............	Mobile.
R. W. Welch	Vice-consul	Key West.
H. R. Kunhardt..................	Consul	New York.
J. H. Gossler	Do...............	Boston.
Charles Kock.....................	Do...............	New Orleans.
Gustav Ziel	Do...............	San Francisco.
Charles Witte	Do...............	Charleston.
August Cohen	Do...............	Philadelphia.
F. Schuster.....................	Do...............	Savannah.
J. F. Meline	Do...............	Cincinnati.
LUBECK.		
F. Kirchoff	Consul	New Orleans.
D. H. Klaener	Do...............	Galveston.
H. von Kapff	Do...............	Baltimore.
J. H. Harjes....................	Do...............	Philadelphia.
H. C. Lauterbach	Do...............	Boston.

15

114 LIST OF FOREIGN CONSULAR OFFICERS, ETC.

Name.	Title.	Residence.
E. F. Stockmeyer	Vice-consul	New Orleans.
C. F. Mebius	Consul	San Francisco.
Geo. C. Voss	Do.	New York.
J. L. H. Thiermann	Do.	Charleston.
Geo. H. Garlichs	Do.	Cincinnati.
BREMEN.		
F. Rodewald	Consul	New Orleans.
A. Schumacher	Consul general	Baltimore.
J. Wolf	Consul	St. Louis.
H. A. H. Runge	Do.	Indianola, Texas.
C. A. C. Duisenberg	Do.	San Francisco.
Gustav Schwab	Do.	New York.
Johannes Schumacher	Do.	Boston.
Edward W. de Voss	Do.	
Johann H. Harjes	Do.	Philadelphia.
Chas. E. Wunderlich	Do.	Charleston.
Julias Kauffmann	Do.	Galveston.
Heinrich Muller	Do.	Savannah.
R. W. Welch	Vice-consul	Key West.
MONACA, Principality of.		
Louis Borg	Consul	New York.
BRAZIL.		
C. Griffin	Vice-consul	New London.
James W. McDonald	Do.	Savannah.
M. Myers	Do.	Norfolk.

LIST OF FOREIGN CONSULAR OFFICERS, ETC. 115

Name.	Title.	Residence.
G. S. Wardwell	Vice-consul	Providence.
H. K. Baldwin	Do.	Richmond.
E. S. Sayres	Do.	Philadelphia.
C. Oliver O'Donnell	Do.	Baltimore.
A. N. Byfield	Do.	San Francisco.
L. H. F. de Aguiar	Consul general	
Archibald Foster	Consul	Boston.
Andrew F. Elliott	Vice-consul	New Orleans.
Oscar G. Parsley	Do.	Wilmington, North Carolina.
C. J. Ludmann	Do.	New York.
Eugene Huchet	Do.	Charleston.
A. T. Kiechoefer	Do.	Washington.
Wm. H. Judah	Do.	Pensacola.
Edwin E. Hertz	Vice-consular agent	Savannah.

MEXICAN REPUBLIC.

Name.	Title.	Residence.
P. J. Marallano	Vice-consul	St. Louis.
C. L. Le Baron	Do.	Mobile.
M. Armendair	Consul	Santa Fé.
J. A. Pizarro	Vice-consul	Baltimore.
F. Merino	Do.	Philadelphia.
J. Herbert	Do.	Pittsburg.
J. I. Castillo	Consul	Brownsville, Texas.
J. E. F. Fallon	Vice-consul	Boston.
W. E. Barron	Do.	San Francisco.
R. de Rafael	Consul	New York.

116 LIST OF FOREIGN CONSULAR OFFICERS, ETC.

Name.	Title.	Residence.
F. Montaner	Vice-consul, *ad interim.*	Charleston.
F. Moreno	Do	Pensacola.
Ricardo Ramires	Vice-consul	Franklin, Texas.
José A. Godoy	Consul	San Francisco.
C. M. Treviño	Do	Brownsville, Texas.
Juan N. Navarro	Consul gen'l, *ad interim.*	New York.
Miguel Zaragoza	Consul	San Antonio de Bexar.
C. F. Gonzalez	Vice-consul	Galveston.
B. A. y Cuevas	Vice-consul, *ad interim.*	New York.
Francisco Riband	Consul general	New Orleans.
Ramon S. Diaz	Consul	New Orleans.
HONDURAS.		
William V. Wells	Consul general	California.
Simon Camacho	Consul	New York.
NICARAGUA.		
O. O'Donnell	Consul	Baltimore.
E. G. Gomez	Do	New Orleans.
Juan J. Barril	Consul general	New York.
José A. Godoy	Consul	San Francisco.
COSTA RICA.		
Royal Phelps	Consul general	New York.
S. M. Waln	Consul	Philadelphia.
E. J. Gomez	Do	Key West.
A. C. Garsia	Do	Boston.
José A. Quintero	Do	New Orleans.

LIST OF FOREIGN CONSULAR OFFICERS, ETC.

Name.	Title.	Residence.
Allan A. Burton	Consul	Louisville, Kentucky.
Gustavo Theisen	Do	New York.
SALVADOR.		
R. W. Heath	Consul	San Francisco.
Jan T. Schepeler	Consul general	
José J. Ribon	Consul	New York.
HAYTI.		
Louis A. de P. Ferrandi	Consul	New York.
Albert Emerson	Do	Bangor, Maine.
B. C. Clark	Do	Boston.
Ellwood Cooper	Consular agent	New York.
George Raster	Consul general	Washington.
DOMINICA.		
José F. Dasora	Consul	New York.
ARGENTINE REPUBLIC.		
N. Frazier	Consul	Philadelphia.
C. M. Stewart	Do	Baltimore.
E. F. Davison	Do	New York.
D. D. Stackpole	Do	Boston.
Andres Spring	Do	Portland.
M. A. Pringle	Do	Charleston.
Carlos Heinsius	Do	Savannah, Ga.
UNITED STATES OF COLOMBIA.		
J. E. Beylle	Consul	New Orleans.
R A. Fisher	Do	Baltimore.

118 LIST OF FOREIGN CONSULAR OFFICERS, ETC

Name.	Title.	Residence.
J. M. R. de Porras	Consul	Philadelphia.
Juan B. Abello	Consul general	New York.
Francisco Herrera	Consul	San Francisco.
S. De Witt Bloodgood	Do	New York.
J. G. Ribon	Vice-consul	New York.
CHILE.		
R. B. Fitzgerald	Consul	Baltimore.
H. V. Ward	Do	Boston.
Enrique Barroilhet	Do	San Francisco.
F. V. Cleeman	Do	Philadelphia.
PERU.		
José Carlos Tracy	Consul	New York.
G. B. Newbery	Do	Boston.
Richard B. Fitzgerald	Do	Baltimore.
Francisco de P. Suarez	Do	Philadelphia.
Enrique Barroilhet	Vice-consul	San Francisco.
Matero Ramirez	Consul	San Francisco.
Adolphe A. Cay	Do.	Charleston.
Arnaldo Marquez	Consul general	New York.
ECUADOR.		
Seth Bryant	Consul	Boston.
J. H. Causten	Do.	Washington.
E. F. Sweetser	Do.	Philadelphia.
C. Ballen	Vice-consul	San Francisco.
Daniel Wolff	Consul	San Francisco.

LIST OF FOREIGN CONSULAR OFFICERS, ETC.

119

Name.	Title.	Residence.
James Gardette	Consul	New Orleans.
Gregorio Dominguez	Do.	New York.
N. R. Ansado	Vice-consul	New York.
ORIENTAL REPUBLIC OF URUGUAY, (Monte Video.)		
C. J. Mansony	Vice-consul	Mobile.
G. L. Lowden	Do.	Charleston.
B. W. Frazier	Do.	Philadelphia.
F. A. Stokes.	Do.	Galveston.
T. P. Hamilton.	Consul	San Francisco.
Carlos E. Leland	Do.	New York.
Charles Soule, jr.	Vice-consul	Boston.
Prudencio Murguiondo	Consul	Baltimore.
A. F. Valls	Vice-consul	New Orleans.
Edwin C. B. Garsia	Consul general	For the United States.
PARAGUAY.		
Richard Mullowney	Consul	New York.
GUATEMALA.		
Bartolomé Blanco	Consul general	New York.
P. Grant	Consul	Boston.
S. M. Waln	Do.	Philadelphia.
Teodoro Manara	Do.	New York.
Guillermo Rabe	Do.	San Francisco.
E. J. Gomez	Do.	New Orleans.
VENEZUELA.		
J. F. Strohm	Consul	Baltimore.

120 LIST OF FOREIGN CONSULAR OFFICERS, ETC.

Name.	Title.	Residence.
S. G. Whitney	Consul	Boston.
G. B. Dieter	Do.	New Orleans.
Leon de la Cova	Do.	Philadelphia.
Florencio Ribas	Do.	New York.
BOLIVIA.		
José M. Muñoz	Consul	New York.
HAWAII, OR SANDWICH ISLANDS.		
Samuel W. F. Odell	Consul general	New York.
H. W. Severance	Consul	San Francisco.
Henry A. Peirce	Do.	Boston.
LIBERIA.		
John B. Pinney	Consul general	New York.
JAPAN.		
Charles W. Brooks	Consul.	San Francisco.